MANNHEIM STEAMROLLER

THE WOLF & THE WARLANDER

THE LONG ROAD

BOOK III

$\mathscr{A}$BOUT $\mathscr{C}$HIP DAVIS

After celebrating the anniversary of releasing a Christmas album that changed the music industry, Chip Davis, founder of the multi-platinum selling group Mannheim Steamroller, reflects on the beginnings of what has become nothing less than an amazing musical journey.

"I remember when I created Mannheim Steamroller Christmas," Davis says of his landmark 1984 album.

"I took it around to all the major buyers and distributors. Back in those days, there were about 20 or 30 independent distributors and hundreds of retail stores and chains. There were a lot of places to go and sell. I remember taking it out and showing it off and playing it for people and the first thing out of their mouths was: *This is a Christmas record; that'll never work!*"

When it comes to the music he has created and the massive audience he has built behind Mannheim Steamroller, Davis has rarely been wrong. From his unlikely base of operations in Omaha, Nebraska, Davis has sold over 40 million records – 27 million in the Christmas genre – making the group one of the top 50 biggest selling musical artists of all time and THE biggest selling Christmas artist of all time.

He's produced hundreds of sold-out Mannheim Steamroller concerts around the world and his American Gramaphone record label stands as one of the most successful independent music franchises in history.

MANNHEIM STEAMROLLER L.L.C.

9130 MORMON BRIDGE ROAD, OMAHA, NE 68152

MANNHEIM STEAMROLLER BOOKS

USA

This book is a work of fiction. Names, characters, places and incidents are products of the author's imagination or are used fictitiously. Any resemblance to actual events or locales or persons, living or dead, is entirely coincidental.

FOR MORE MANNHEIM STEAMROLLER
MUSIC PRODUCTS, BOOKS AND CONCERT TOUR SCHEDULES
VISIT OUR WEBSITE
WWW.MANNHEIMSTEAMROLLER.COM
OR CALL US AT 402.457.4341

STORY BY CHIP DAVIS

WRITTEN BY MARK VALENTI

ILLUSTRATIONS BY JAMES TAYLOR

PACKAGE DESIGN BY JAMES TAYLOR

PACKAGE PHOTO BY BRIAN ARNOLD

LAYOUT BY JEANNE JOHNSON

A SPECIAL THANKS TO

MANNHEIM STEAMROLLER STAFF

To My Family

KELLY, EVAN, ELYSE

MANNHEIM STEAMROLLER

THE WOLF & THE WARLANDER

THE FOREVER TIME

BOOK III

One

Ghost stood atop a high ridge overlooking the valley where he and Echo had raised their family. Happy memories flooded his mind; when his first offspring was born, carefree times when they romped with each other. The valley had been a deeply happy place for him. Echo promised to make his life complete and she had done exactly that. She was completely devoted to Ghost. In return, Ghost provided her and their brood with a safe, warm and happy home.

As herd elder, Ghost spent as much time as possible with the youngest horses, offering them encouragement and answering their endless questions. He wanted to be an example for them to follow, as his father had been for him. Now that he had grown old, Ghost thought more often about leaving something meaningful behind for those who would come after him. He had no great riches to offer, but he did have a lifetime of experiences and stories, passed on from his father, that he could share.

And so Ghost invited the young ones to gather near him every afternoon, underneath an apple tree. There, he would tell them stories about their Warlander ancestors – how they rode bravely into battle, and how they showed fierce loyalty to the soldiers they carried. The young horses were amazed to hear their own kind had taken part in such terrible fights; their own lives were peaceful and carefree, not at all troubled by such matters as war and conflict.

Ghost didn't dwell on the fighting when he told his stories. He wanted the young ones to know their history, and the ancestors who kept the Warlander traits alive and the countries they visited. Ghost felt it was important for these stories to be passed down from one generation to the next. If you know where you come from, you can better determine where you're going.

As was his usual habit, Ghost stood beneath the apple tree and neighed loudly, calling the younger horses to gather around. Within seconds, they began arriving, their enthusiasm indicating these stories were a favorite pastime for them. They struggled to stand as close as possible to Ghost.

Everybody settle down, you'll all be able to hear the story! Ghost laughed to himself; it was a good feeling to know that the horses were so interested in hearing his tales.

Can you tell us about your father winning The Running four times?

Many of the horses made sounds of agreement with this request.

No! Let's hear the story about the Warlander who traveled to America across a great ocean!

This idea was greeted with equal amounts of agreement from the other horses. Ghost thought it over.

How about if I tell you a new story, one you haven't heard before?

All of the horses let out excited responses.

All right. As it was told to me, this happened hundreds of years ago. That's a very long time, isn't it? I'm not saying that what I'm about to tell you really happened; it's up to you to decide whether you believe it or not.

But one thing is true: the horse I'm going to tell you about was just like you. Young, eager to do big things, strong and capable. Now, horses back then had the same desires and needs we have today – to eat, drink and live in a safe place. We need friendship and family. But this horse, named Thoren, wanted something no other horse had ever wanted before. He dreamed of being able to fly.

The young horses gathered around let out excited oohs and aahs.

Everybody knows a horse can't fly!

Yeah! Why did he waste his time fooling around with a dream like that?

Because he did learn how to fly.

What?! That's impossible!

You need to listen because Thoren proved that nothing is impossible to a horse with courage, imagination and a little bit of luck. Thoren used to watch the birds flying overhead; he loved how they soared and dove, let the wind carry them, or fluttered

*their wings, to hold steady in the sky. It all seemed like magic to
him. In fact, he loved the birds so much that he used to climb
the highest mountains, rising far above the clouds, just so he
could feel what it was like to be a bird.*

Horses are too heavy to fly!

And they don't have any wings!

*That's all true. But a clever horse doesn't need wings to fly.
Here's what Thoren did. Once, when he was standing on top of
that very high mountain, the wind started to blow – gently at
first and then stronger and harder, until Thoren found it very
difficult to even stand up straight. He tried to climb back down,
but some boulders became dislodged and the pathway down to
the valley was blocked. A dangerous thunderstorm started
coming near; the winds were getting stronger – so strong that
they knocked over a tree that had been standing on top of that
mountain for hundreds of years. It came crashing down next to
Thoren, barely missing him!*

*Suddenly, lightning and thunder erupted all around. Rain
poured down like a waterfall and the ground beneath Thoren's
feet became loose and unstable. The great tree that had fallen
was being battered by the winds, whipped to and fro as if some
great giant was shaking it. Finally an impossibly strong gust of
wind knocked Thoren off his feet; he landed sideways atop the
thick, leafy branches of the tree.*

*And that's when the most astonishing thing happened…the
wind pushed the tree off the mountain, with Thoren on top of
it! The tree became caught up in a fierce tornado, spinning*

crazily, round and round, until it somehow escaped the vortex and flew across the sky, kept aloft by the strong winds!

There he was, flying across the sky on top of that tree, rising to his feet and feeling the wind blowing back his mane. He understood the danger, make no mistake. It didn't take much thinking to understand that falling from such a high altitude could prove deadly to him when that tree struck the ground!

But he didn't care. No, he wasn't concerned about the danger, or the pain, or anything else other than the fact that he – Thoren, a mere horse – was flying like the greatest of the winged creatures that had ever graced the skies!

Somehow that tree was kept in the sky for one minute, then two minutes, then five! Down below, Thoren's friends watched from the safety of a cave – nobody could believe what they were seeing!

Slowly, the storm passed, the winds died down and that giant tree floated to the ground, Thoren atop it, a look of pride and amazement on his face. He stepped off the branches onto solid ground and was met with great cheers from the horses that had come out to celebrate his incredible feat.

The young horses were speechless; they stared at Ghost with their mouths open.

That's the story as it was told to me, and that's the story you'll tell your children.

One of the young horses finally spoke.

Is it true? Did it really happen?

A story doesn't have to be true to be true, if you know what

I mean.

I'm not sure...

Let's just think of it like this: a horse doesn't need wings to fly and a tall tale can teach you just as much as a true one.

So it wasn't true?

Oh, I didn't say that.

So it is true?

I didn't say that either. But it's an important story because it shows that you can do anything if you believe in yourself with all of your heart. Even the most impossible things.

Ghost, did you ever do anything amazing?

Yeah! Tell us about something you did that was like flying!

Ghost smiled at the insistent questions.

Well, my life has been a little different. My father became ill, so I had to stay near home to help care for my mother.

So you never had an adventure?

It's not that, I...

Ghost was suddenly overwhelmed with the same longing he felt as a young horse, when he wanted to race into the world and have adventures in every country. He was left with a feeling of emptiness, of unfulfilled dreams that simply vanished along the way.

Let's meet again tomorrow. We'll have another story then.

But...

Go on, now. Don't waste all that sunshine, go out and run!

The young horses obeyed the command, turning and cantering into a meadow where they could run freely. Ghost watched them and wondered how many of them had the same kinds of dreams he had when he was young. Do they dream of adventure? Do they want to see the world, as I did? Will their dreams die, as mine did?

———

Seti moved through the forest slowly, pausing to sniff the air every now and then. There were rabbits to his north; most likely a family taking refuge in their warren after having spotted him coming. He lifted his head and closed his eyes; another scent came to him from the west but he couldn't quite identify it. Cougar? No, this was more insistent; a deeper, muskier smell. He opened his mouth and took a deep breath. It's not mountain lion…what animal could it be?

Seti opened his eyes and sat back on his haunches. This was the third time in recent weeks that his senses had failed him. When he was young, his nose was incapable of making a mistake; he could identify a predator from a mile away.

Now, as age descended on him, he was beginning to feel less skilled. As a hunter, and leader of his pack, it was very important for him to remain strong in every way. Maybe these recent failures were just a minor and short-term problem. He would redouble his efforts to eat properly, get plenty of sleep, and make sure he was in top physical shape.

He turned to head back toward home when suddenly he was attacked from the side by an unknown creature that head-butted him! It didn't hurt at all, but it did take him by surprise. He barely had time to look to his left when he was hit on his other side! Suddenly, Seti was being pummeled – rather softly – by attacks from every direction!

When he finally gathered his thoughts and looked around, he saw that his young grandsons were playfully butting into him, pretending to attack a predator!

As Seti maneuvered to a more advantageous position, he saw that his grandsons were all covered in thick mud to hide their scent – just as he had taught them.

Don't stop now, boys! Bring down this terrible beast!

The oldest of his grandsons, Raff, rust-red-haired and extremely energetic, led the charge. He leapt toward Seti with his paws outstretched and managed to land a decent blow to his grandfather's flank. Seti countered by lowering his body, sending Raff sailing head over tail into a sticky bramble behind them.

Ow! Grandfather, get me out! Help me!

Seti hurried to the bramble and stepped on some branches, allowing Raff to scamper out of the pointy branches. Raff shook furiously from head to toe, sending flakes of mud flying in all directions.

Careful, Raff, or we'll all have to take an extra bath today!

Raff looked up at Seti eagerly.

Were you surprised? Did we sneak up on you?

You did indeed.

Yes!

Raff exulted, bouncing into the air, crashing into his siblings and cousins.

You learned to cover your scent well, Raff. You all did. But how did you know that I would go easy on you when you attacked me? How did you know I wouldn't bite your head off while you were still in the air?

Because you're our grandfather!

Ahh, but when a wolf is being attacked, he is no one's grandfather, or brother or son. He is a fierce and proud hunter who will defend his territory and life at all costs.

Then how come you didn't...uh...bite my head off?

The truth? Because I am old and slow.

You're not! You're Seti, greatest of the great! The strongest, bravest wolf that ever lived!

The other young wolves howled their agreement. Seti chuckled.

Well, this morning, the greatest of the great feels a little tired. Come on, all of you, let's go down to the lake and clean off this mud. Then we'll play a game of keep away. What do you say?

Last one in the lake is a dog!

Raff led the way as the young pups charged at full speed down the pathway and out of sight.

Seti straightened himself, feeling tender in his flank where the pups had hit him.

Raff has fire in his eyes, that's for sure....

Back in the compound, Seti found his first-born son,

Ramses, standing near his sleeping area, as if waiting for his father to return.

Ramses, I thought you were leading the hunt today.

We've already gone and returned. There's elk meat in the preserve.

I've asked you to leave that herd alone, son. Their numbers are dwindling and they can't survive without a boost in their numbers.

Why should we care if they survive? They're food. Nothing more.

You know better than that. When you were young I taught you about nature's balance. Old growth forests give way to new, but that can't happen unless they're able to establish firm roots so the soil can bear the new generation. It's the same with –

I know, Father, you've told me this a thousand times!

Seti was taken aback by Ramses' rudeness.

Do not take that tone with me.

Ramses hung his head, stung by Seti's reprimand. But within an instant, he was again filled with fire.

Last winter? When we lost two of our own elders for lack of food? We could have easily kept them alive, but you wouldn't let the pack hunt to the north! And why? Because you said the wildlife there was trying to survive, the same as us! Well, isn't that the point? We're all trying to survive! We all need to eat! So why pass up a perfectly good kill? Our bellies are hungry now! By next year, we may all be dead!

Seti watched Ramses closely. There was something more

to his anger than mere hunting rules.

What is really bothering you, son?

Ramses averted Seti's gaze, instead staring onto the horizon. Beyond the inner ring of trees that protected the herd against the weather, there was a vast forest and, beyond that, rocky mountains that seemed to go on a million miles.

I'm leaving.

Leaving…where?

I'm old enough to run my own pack. I have ideas about how to be a successful pack leader, and it's time for me to try.

Ramses, being pack leader isn't something you wish for yourself. It takes years. Working your way through the ranks, demonstrating to the other wolves that you are not only trustworthy, but that you have the wisdom to lead them through every kind of challenge imaginable.

The old ways…they're not…helpful any more.

You mean my ways?

Well, Father, if you want to put it like that. Yes. The world is much more dangerous than when you were young. Predators are everywhere. Our territory is shrinking, humans are invading our acreage. Besides, wolves don't want to be dominated by other animals. We should take our rightful place and exert our will over them all.

Seti was puzzled by this kind of talk from his son. He had always known Ramses was prone to be emotional. He had behaved in thoughtless, warlike ways in the past. But Seti believed that Ramses was just young, perhaps immature and he would grow out of his troublemaking. Now it seemed that Ramses' darker nature had found a permanent home in his heart.

Son, I've seen wolves live only for the kind of anguish they can make in the lives of others. Wolves that prowl the countryside, destroying dens, committing senseless slaughter.

That's not what I'm talking about!

But that's the result of where you are heading!

Father, your own leadership has been attacked a dozen times, from right here within our own pack!

But who is still leader?

You've allowed wolves to insult you and then walk away without facing any consequences.

What would you have done? Killed any wolf who dared call you a name?

That's what leaders do!

No. That's what animals do when they are sick in the head.

Ramses stood, frozen with anger. He fought the impulse to respond, knowing that anything he would say would be extremely harsh – even unforgivable. Instead, he calmed himself and inhaled deeply.

I…I'll be gone by sunset. I'm only taking two others with me – I don't want to leave you defenseless. I've already said goodbye to Mother.

What about your son? What about Raff?

He'll be fine. When I've established my pack I'll come back for him.

Seti was silent. His mind raced with images of Ramses at

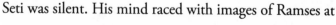

various stages in his life – when he was born, when he joined the pack for the first time, when he nearly drowned in the river. Ramses had been a good, loving son. Now, here he was, filled with a dark worldview that seemed to have no boundaries.

Is there anything I can say to change your mind?

No.

Then…go with courage and strength.

They held their gaze for a moment; Ramses bowed his head slightly, a final gesture of respect, then turned and ran into the forest.

———

Ghost and his son, Rider, galloped next to each other, matching stride for stride, filling their lungs with air and pushing each other to their greatest effort. Running next to his son made Ghost feel like a young colt again. He could feel Rider pulling ahead and knew he was slowing down slightly in order to allow his father to remain by his side. Ghost was pleased by this; his son was showing him consideration and respect, everything a father could ask for from a son.

They continued their run along a dusty trail, sending huge billowing clouds behind them. Their hoof beats thumped in a regular pattern and Ghost could feel his own heart beat matching their rhythm.

Finally, they reached a watering hole in a small valley

surrounded by wildflowers. Ghost was winded and he could feel his muscles tightening. Tomorrow he would wake up in pain. But today, he was happy.

I wish your brother would join us on these runs.

Sky says he's not about to waste energy doing something silly like running for no reason. He'd rather laze in the sun. In fact, he's become an expert in that activity.

I love Sky just the same as I love you and your sister. But I would like to see him take on some responsibility. You were helping me herd the younger horses when you were barely grown yourself.

Sky will find his way, Father. He's smart and would do anything to avoid letting you down.

Except work hard. Or run with us. Or wake up with the sunrise.

Right!

They both shared a laugh at Sky's lack of initiative. Ghost wondered how long it would be before his younger son finally stepped up and started his journey toward becoming the horse he was meant to be.

Back home, Echo and her daughter Dancer were returning from feeding on clover on the south meadow. Dancer was lovely, like her mother, with a white patch on her forehead that resembled a star. Her coat was grayish brown with flecks of white scattered throughout and her mane was cloud-white.

Mother, if I can convince Sky to come with me, may I go to

the eastern ridge today? Some of my friends are going to be there and they said a flock of hundreds of geese has settled in the valley there.

I thought we discussed you helping me at the orchard. Those apples will spoil if we let them rot on the ground.

Dancer lowered her head, disappointed.

You're right, I did promise to help you.

Echo looked at her daughter with loving eyes.

I suppose the apples can wait one more day.

Dancer lifted her head and stared at her mother.

Oh thank you, Mother! We won't be gone long and I'll wake up extra early tomorrow morning to help you with the apples!

Dancer nuzzled Echo with her nose and galloped away to find Sky.

Ghost and Echo were on the ridge, watching the sun set – their favorite way to end the day. Echo stared at her mate, noticing that he hadn't spoken for most of the day. Sometimes when he was silent, it meant he was thinking about his parents and his days as a young horse. But this felt different – she could tell he had something troubling on his mind.

Is there anything you'd like to share with me?

Hmm? Oh…no, I'm sorry. I was just lost in thought.

Are you sure?

Yes, I'm… Well, actually there is something on my mind.

Echo turned to give him her full attention.

Let's talk about it. Maybe I can help.

Ghost exhaled deeply. He gazed toward the horizon as he spoke.

The other day, when I was telling stories to the young ones – they wanted to know about the adventures I've had in my life.

Oh no, Ghost, you didn't tell them frightening stories, did you?

Not at all. I couldn't tell them anything because I've never had any adventures.

Dear one, your life has been full of adventure! Raising our children, finding our home, even the sad times with your parents.

It's not the same. When I was young, I wanted so much to go off and see the world, know what it was like out there, beyond the horizon. I wanted to travel in the same footsteps as my ancestors. To taste the challenges; to brave the elements. Instead, I've spent most of my time telling stories to youngsters.

Echo nuzzled him with her forehead.

I've never met a braver horse than you. Why, even standing up to my father the way you did was far more courageous than anything I've seen!

Echo, I'm grateful for our life together. Please don't think I'm questioning that in any way. It's just that I…I've always felt that I could have done more, seen more of the world. Well… never mind. It's just a passing feeling.

Echo stared into Ghost's eyes. They didn't have the same sparkle she had grown used to seeing. Her heart ached at the thought of her beloved mate being so unhappy.

The children are grown. Our lives are easy here, you've seen to that. I want you to make a plan and then go off on that grand adventure.

Ghost turned to look at Echo. He could scarcely believe his ears.

I…I can't leave you. How foolish it would be for me to be that selfish! Actually it would be worse than foolish! It could be dangerous!!

I know you, my dear. You are old and wise, but you have the heart of a child. You see beauty in rainfall and adventure in the night sky. And you will never be truly satisfied until you are able to come home and tell me stories about the amazing world you've seen. And nothing would make me happier than to hear you share those stories.

But…it would mean leaving you here by yourself…for a long time.

We have three children, plus many grandchildren. I would be no more alone than a bee in a hive.

Ghost gulped. It was one thing to dream about an adventure, but quite another to actually go out and find one.

Echo, are you sure?

I am. And now is a good time – you've got all of spring and summer ahead of you.

What if…what if I'm gone longer?

Every night I'll look at the stars and trust that you are resting your head safely under them as well. Just promise me one thing?

Anything!

Take Seti with you.

———

Sky! Sky, wake up!

Dancer stood over her brother, who was snoring loudly,

lying on his side on top of dust and hay. When he didn't respond to her cries, she lifted her foreleg and held it against his nose, forcing him to breathe through a single nostril. He snorted and let out a gasp, lifting his head.

Hey! What are you trying to do, kill me?

No, I'm trying to wake you up!

Sky, grumbling under his breath, slowly rose to his feet and shook his body. A dust cloud erupted, making Dancer cough.

What's so important you have to wake me up in the middle of a nap?

Mother wants you to come with me to the eastern ridge. My friends are going to see the geese!

Sky cocked his head at his sister.

No thanks!

And with that, Sky lowered himself back to the ground and closed his eyes.

Dancer exhaled sharply and took a step forward, directly onto Sky's tail.

Ow!

Sky once again rose to his feet, angry.

I'm not joining you and your silly friends while you look at birds you can see in the sky any day of the year!

If you don't go with me, I can't go, so that's why you're going with me!

I'm not!

Mother probably wanted you to come because you need

the exercise.

Very funny. Go away.

Please, Sky! If you don't come with me, I can't go!

After a moment, Sky exhaled sharply. He rose to his feet.

Fine. I'll go. But you owe me a big favor, probably two or three! And you can clean up my sleeping area for me! And I get all of your extra apples for the next week!

Dancer just nodded and laughed as they made their way to the eastern ridge, with Sky continuing his litany of favors.

—⁓—

For the past week, Seti would glance at the horizon, hoping to see Ramses running back home again. But in his heart, he knew Ramses was far too headstrong to come home so soon. He would rather starve than admit he was wrong. That stubbornness was something Seti both admired and disliked about his son. On the one hand, Ramses was a warrior who would never give up. But on the other hand, the young wolf could sometimes fail to understand very important principles – ones that would have made his life far easier.

Ramses was strong – of that there was no doubt. But Seti always felt his son's stubbornness was an indication of fear. Seti believed that Ramses sometimes covered up that fear by behaving harsher and more aggressively than a situation might warrant. And this latest move by Ramses – leaving the pack to start his own – seemed like one more action designed to make him seem more of a leader than he really was.

Seti and Luna had discussed Ramses often over the years. There were times when their son made them feel so proud – like when he stopped to help a fallen friend during a race, or when he gave up some of his meal to feed one of the elderly wolves.

But now, with Ramses leaving and with his headstrong behavior filling Seti and Luna with concern, they were more certain than ever their beloved son had made the mistake of his life. They wished there was something they could do or say that would make him come back home. But in truth, they had done all they could to raise him properly. Now, it was up to Ramses to learn on his own.

As Seti turned back toward home, he saw a familiar figure galloping through the forest, along the path the wolves had worn through repeated crossings. Seti raced to meet him before the younger wolves saw the tall horse; they would have been afraid because of his size and some of them may have attacked Ghost, since they were still unaware how to control their deepest wolf instincts.

Ghost, how great to see you, old friend!

I hope I haven't come at a bad time, Seti!

Not at all! Come, let's go to our Talking Place.

The two friends walked casually through the forest to a clearing, where they had been meeting privately for the past few years. They learned long ago when they visited each other at their homes, the rest of the animals became nervous or fearful. Neither of them wanted to cause these kinds of disruptions, so they had chosen a spot, deep in the woods, where they could spend as much time as they wanted, just the two of them, talking and sharing stories.

When they reached the Talking Place, they both settled into their respective spots – Ghost taking his rest near some edible moss, and Seti, curled up on the cool forest floor. Ghost spoke first.

How is the family? I was hoping to catch a glimpse of Luna.

She's fine, we are all moving a little slower these days, but you know Luna, nothing can bring her down for long.

And the children?

Seti looked away, thinking of Ramses.

Mostly good. My boy is giving me some concern.

It's his age. They all do that.

I hope it's just a passing phase. I have great hopes for him.

With you as his father, I'm sure he'll be fine. It may take a little extra time.

The grandchildren are keeping me busy. Just the other day, they attacked me!

Soon, you and I will be the slowest and the weakest in our families. Which brings me to the reason I've come to visit you. Do you remember when we were young and we spoke about going into the world and having grand adventures?

Of course. It was all we talked about. You wanted to visit the land of your ancestors and I was going to travel all around the world. Those were nice dreams, weren't they?

Yes, but they can be more than dreams.

How?

We are both still alive, still breathing. Why don't we do what we dreamed of doing so long ago?

You mean go off and have an adventure?

Exactly!

I think maybe you skipped breakfast, Ghost. Or you haven't been getting enough sleep. That's a perfectly crazy idea.

No, it isn't! What is traveling, anyway? It's putting one foot in front of the other, just as we do now. The only difference is we don't keep walking in circles, we go in a straight line until we reach a wonderful new place!

And what do you propose we do about our families?

Echo has told me its fine with her as long as you came along with me.

I don't think Luna would react the same way. Especially now.

What is different about now?

Seti lowered his head and closed his eyes.

My son has left to begin his own pack.

That's good, isn't it? Going off on his own?

No, my friend. I'm afraid Ramses has some very bad ideas about what it means to be an alpha male. He seeks trouble where there is none and prefers fighting to talking.

Oh Seti, I'm sure Ramses will come around. Just give him time.

I'm worried about him, Ghost. Truly worried. I couldn't

*even think about leaving home as long as my heart is heavy
with sadness over his behavior.*

*I understand. Well, I'm sad for you, Seti. I know how much
you love that boy.*

*Thank you, Ghost. And I'm sorry I can't join you. I hope
you find a way to reach your adventures, even if it's without me.*

———

Dancer raced along a rocky ledge, whipping past
branches, leaping over ruts on the path. She was full of
excitement about joining her friends to see the geese. She
only hoped she wasn't too late – her brother Sky had
dawdled as they had crossed the meadow, complaining every
step of the way. She would race ahead and then have to wait
for him to catch up to her. Their journey was taking twice as
long as it used to!

Dancer paused, not turning around. She didn't want to
give Sky the satisfaction of knowing she was waiting for
him. Instead, she watched two butterflies fluttering near
some coneflowers, favorite of the little flying creatures. How
delicately they moved around each other until they landed
on the colorful plants, their beautifully detailed wings slowly
opening and closing.

Eventually, she heard hooves behind her – slow and
plodding.

I'm tired! Let's stop here and rest!

Sky was neither winded nor particularly tired, Dancer

thought. In fact, he looked pretty well rested to her.

The eastern ridge is just a few minutes away. Come on!

You keep saying that, but we keep walking!!

But she was already trotting along the path. Soon, she rounded a corner and was out of sight.

Exasperated, Sky let out a groan and continued along the path. When he came to the corner, he heard low growling. He stepped forward carefully and saw that Dancer was being held at bay by three snarling wolves!

Dancer, come on! Let's run!

They would catch us...

That's right. We would catch you!

The lead wolf snarled and bared his fangs. It was Ramses.

You are crossing our territory. That was not very smart.

Dancer's heart was racing.

This is not wolf territory! We have been coming this way for many years!

No longer.

Ramses took a step forward.

Wait, I know you! Your father and my father are friends! You are Ramses!

Ramses paused and looked around quickly at the two other wolves.

I...I don't know how you know my name, but you are wrong! No wolf is a friend to a horse!

Of course they are! I've seen your father in the woods with my father! They've been friends for many years.

The two wolves with Ramses started to grumble. Ramses took another menacing step forward.

Stop with your lies!

He leapt forward, but before he could reach Dancer, Sky pushed her out of the way and leaned in to absorb the blow from the young wolf. Ramses bit into Sky's shoulder, causing the young horse to rear back on his hind legs in pain.

Dancer, run! Go now!

I'm not going to leave you!

The other two wolves moved forward, alongside Ramses, who licked the blood from his mouth.

No one can defeat the power of the wolf! We are kings of the forest!

With that, he let out a loud howl – it was the death cry, the precursor to what would surely be a horrible death for both horses.

Sky and Dancer stood frozen, not knowing what to do. But in an instant – their answer came.

Attracted by the sound of the wolves' cry, another pack of wolves – older, larger and weathered by years in the elements – erupted from the thick stand of trees. The lead wolf, its coat filled with bite marks and matted fur, quickly assessed the situation, seeing both horses.

Good of you to prepare our meal for us, young ones!

Ramses' neck fur bristled and he showed his fangs.

They belong to us!

We'll see about that!

The older pack attacked Ramses and the other two wolves with a fury that caused Dancer to hold her breath in alarm. Never before had she seen such a terrible sight; it was as if the wolves were possessed by demons!

Sky nudged Dancer and indicated she should back away from the scene very slowly. They both did so, and as they rounded the corner of the path, they began galloping as fast as they could go.

Seti's head was low, near the water. He paused to take a drink from a small brook, but when he finished, he found it impossible to look away from his reflection. It was as if he was frozen in place. He stared at his reflected image, poring over his features. His muzzle was grey; his eyes dark. He could see the scar that ran down the side of his neck – fur would no longer grow there. The bite that had produced the scar came from his own father, rabid and half-crazed, before he died on a cold, wet winter day.

Suddenly, Seti's reflection was replaced by that of his son, Ramses, and Seti felt a stab of pain in his stomach that caused him to fall to the muddy ground. His entire body felt as if it was on fire, and he writhed uncontrollably, unable to breathe, his eyes rolling back in his head. A low moan escaped from his mouth completely out of his control.

After a moment, the pain stopped. Seti gasped for air

and fought to regain his footing. He was overwhelmed with a feeling of dread.

As he came to his senses, his instinct told him to return home as quickly as possible! Without thinking, Seti began running faster than he had ever run before. He took huge gulps of air, his lungs filling, as his paws dug into the earth, propelling him forward. Branches whipped his face as he moved, but he felt nothing.

Finally he arrived at the cliffs overlooking his home. Instead of running down the winding path, he leaped through the air and landed on the mossy grass where he slept each night.

All was quiet. He moved toward his sleeping area, and there he saw Luna, on her side, weeping uncontrollably.

He ran to her.

Luna! What is it?

She gazed at him helplessly. She didn't need to say a word. He knew.

It's Ramses...he's...

Luna closed her eyes and buried her head in her chest fur. Seti fell to the ground as if something had knocked the wind out of him. He was suddenly aware he was being watched. He looked into the meadow and saw that the wolves of his pack were standing together, some distance a way, respectful of Seti's sadness. He gulped, stunned with the awful realization that his beloved son, who had filled his heart with such love and pride, would never stand among those wolves again.

All that night and the next day, Luna was inconsolable. She wouldn't eat or sleep and did not stir from her position on the ground. Seti however, being leader of the pack, went through the motions of his responsibilities, dead inside.

He had been told by the wolves, who joined Ramses in his ill-fated bid to create his own pack, that his son had foolishly wandered into unknown territory without first investigating the area to discover potential dangers. As it happened, Ramses had been threatening the lives of two young horses when he was attacked by marauder wolves, who had staked out that place as their own. Apparently Ramses had put up a valiant fight. When it became obvious the marauder wolves would easily defeat them, his two friends called out for Ramses to retreat to safety.

But Ramses couldn't do that. He was utterly convinced his strength and determination would defeat the wolves. Even when the lead wolf had him bleeding on the ground, insisting that Ramses beg for mercy, he wouldn't stop fighting. Ramses gave up his final chance to surrender, and the wolves descended on him.

Seti refused an offer by the wolves to show him the spot where his son fell. He didn't want to have that image fixed in his mind. Instead, he would choose to recall his son in his younger days, when he was carefree and full of hope.

Seti had learned, through many punishing events in his life, that strength and power were tools to be used for the benefit of all. The moment they were turned against another for personal gain, they became burdens – sins that would have to be somehow blotted out of one's soul. Ramses, despite Seti's teachings, somehow never heard that lesson, much less adopted it into his heart. He believed there was only one way for a wolf to live and it had cost him his life.

Three

That is terrible news!

Echo reacted to the tale being shared by Dancer and Sky. Even worse than the danger they faced by a wolf attack was the fact that Seti's own son had started the whole incident.

What is terrible news?

Ghost ambled toward his family after completing his morning run. He was surprised to find Dancer, Rider – and even Sky – awake and talking with their mother.

Oh Father, it was so frightening!

Dancer turned toward Ghost. He could see the fear had not yet left her eyes.

But you should have seen how Sky defended me!

Defended you against what?

Echo sidled next to her mate.

It's not good, dear. The children were attacked in the forest by a pack of wolves. And the lead wolf was Ramses, Seti's son.

What?!

Ghost couldn't believe what he was hearing. The last time he saw Ramses, the boy was a mere pup, full of enthusiasm and mischief. He recalled how Seti had gently guided his son away from a nearby hillside only to see him return again and again to the danger spot. Finally, Seti allowed Ramses to get one step too close, so that the young pup rolled down the hill and landed in a swamp. Sputtering and gasping for air, Ramses found his feet and scrambled out of the mess, exclaiming loudly that it wasn't his fault, but it was Seti's for not stopping him.

Is everyone all right?

Ghost moved closer to his offspring. He saw a bite mark on Sky's shoulder.

I'm fine, Father. It doesn't hurt.

It would have been me, if Sky hadn't stepped in! He saved my life!

Ghost stared at his son.

I'm proud of you.

Sky looked away, embarrassed.

It was nothing.

No. It was everything.

Later, after the young horses finished telling their story and had gone to forage for their meal, Ghost and Echo made themselves comfortable in their sleep area. Ghost had a feeling of pride.

It seems that our son has started to find himself.

Just as you knew he would, Ghost.

But what a sad turn of events for Seti! I know how he loved that boy and how hard he tried to teach him the proper ways

of the wolf. Seti was worried about him. I'm afraid that some
wolves are simply too dangerous to reason with.

Your father said wolves were insane creatures.

And yet he changed his mind when he met Seti.

Perhaps Seti is the odd one. Perhaps wolves will never be
agreeable to most animal life.

I suppose so…

Suddenly, Echo whipped her head toward the meadow.

Ghost – look!

In the distance, standing rock-still at the edge of the
meadow was Seti.

What is he doing?

Ghost rose to his feet.

I'll go see.

Ghost cantered across the meadow until he reached his
old friend. Seti looked weary and defeated; his eyes were
dull and his coat was dirty.

Seti, are you all right?

No, Ghost. My son…

I know. The children told me that he…well, that he was
behaving…

He's dead. My son is dead.

Oh no…Seti, how did it happen?

He died the way he lived. Violently and senselessly. I've
come to ask your forgiveness for his attack on your children. I
hope they're all right…

They're fine, Seti! And there's no need for you to apologize, you had no idea...

I...I did my best with him...but there was just no...no way to...

Seti fell to the ground, inconsolable. Ghost knelt down beside him as his friend let out a howl of pain and sadness that filled the meadow and the valley beyond. It was the most tragic sound Ghost had ever heard, and it seemed to go on forever.

That night, the two friends remained at each other's side, saying nothing. Ghost kept a watchful eye on Seti, for fear he would rush away and do something damaging to himself. But Seti had no energy for that; he was lifeless and still.

The next morning, Rider approached them and asked his father if there was anything they needed.

No, son. Thank you.

Just then, Seti lifted his head and looked at Rider.

You are Ghost's first-born?

Yes, sir.

Be strong for your father always. Live up to his expectations for you. But most importantly, find yourself. Know who you are. Walk through this life for others, as your father does.

Rider nodded. His eyes met Ghost's – Ghost nodded back to him.

I'll...I'll go see if Mother needs anything. I'm sorry for your son.

With that, Rider galloped out of the meadow. Seti watched him, then rose to his feet. His eyes had a faraway look.

He's a good son, Ghost.

So was Ramses, Seti. He was just misguided.

Don't say that. Ramses did it to himself. We have to speak the truth, or else the truth doesn't matter. Your son gives me hope. I know it's possible to be good in this world without any hope of reward. To be good and fair and decent for no other reason but that it's the best way to be. Yesterday I was filled with despair. Today my faith has been rekindled.

Seti turned to face Ghost.

Do you still want to go on that adventure with me?

Ghost was surprised by the question.

You mean…what I asked you about a while ago?

Yes. I spoke to Luna. She knows that if I stay home my heart will be filled with sadness and dark thoughts of what might have been. She told me to come see you, to see the world and find myself again.

Well, Seti, that's…that's wonderful! When can we leave?

How about today?

———

Ghost and Seti had agreed to remain hidden from the main roads for fear of being spotted by humans. They had already discussed the hazards they would encounter on their journey and identified humans as their greatest threat.

Humans did not understand wolves and therefore were determined to kill as many of them as possible. And horses, to humans, were mere creatures of work, to be captured, broken and trained to perform mindless – and seemingly endless – tasks of burden.

So the two friends spent most of their time in the first few days racing through fields and behind trees to avoid being seen. It was freeing in a way, especially for Seti, because he could simply run and run, without having to think about anything. Of course, Ramses was in his heart at all times, but seeing new lands and rushing headlong into unfamiliar places was healing.

Ghost told Seti about the ancestors that had come from far away. There was a great body of water – called an ocean – and huge ships, carrying humans, food and many other things, had sailed on those waters. That's how Ghost's ancestors had arrived in this part of the world.

Ghost recounted how his ancestors had fought in great battles, braving cannon fire and soldiers on horseback carrying sharp weapons. The horses withstood every attack and refused to leave the side of their humans.

Seti reminded Ghost that humans could be cruel. Ghost needed no reminder; his abuse at the hands of humans several years ago had left him nearly blinded and crippled. Still, Ghost believed there were good and bad humans, just as there were good and bad horses. He did not want to live his life fearing anyone or anything; he would look for the best and deal with whatever came his way.

At night, the two friends sought a place to settle where

they would be protected on at least two sides by brush or
terrain. A horse and a wolf would present a confusing
picture to predators who might strike first without
bothering to assess the danger of the situation.

The night air was colder now; summer had given way to
autumn and with it came stronger winds and more frequent
rainfall. Mature trees offered them the greatest protection
against the weather, but it was hard to travel effectively
through the forest, with its numerous barriers and
uncertain pathways.

All Ghost knew was they had to continue to travel in
the direction of the sunrise. That was where his father had
told him the ocean was. And so every morning, he and Seti
roused themselves, ate what food they could find and set out
for another day of travel. They would run for several hours,
then walk more slowly until they regained their energy, then
once again they would run. This gave them the chance to
travel for miles every day.

As they headed east, they noticed the daylight hours
were getting colder, not just the nighttime. An early blast of
winter weather – if it was strong enough – could slow their
progress and make it more difficult to reach their
destination.

One night, as a cold wind howled, Ghost and Seti
sought shelter in a small cave. There was just enough room
for Ghost's tall body; Seti, using his excellent night vision,
had determined the cave was empty, and there were no

predators lurking.

I didn't think it would be so cold.

Ghost shivered and stamped his feet.

As long as we keep moving, we'll be fine.

Seti stretched out, curled against the cave's rear wall. He felt secure as the strong winds continued blowing outside.

Ghost, I've made up my mind about something. After what happened to Ramses and taking into account what it means to be a wolf, the things that we do, the way we live our lives…

Ghost settled his body up against the same rear wall and listened intently.

Well, I've come to a decision. I will never be violent again, no matter what happens.

What do you mean, Seti? You're a wolf! You'll have to defend yourself. And honestly, if you want to eat, you'll be forced into violent situations.

All I know is that my son would still be alive if he had chosen a different path. And there have been many times in my own life when violence was the only choice I thought I had — but that wasn't true.

You've told me many times about the balance of nature, about how every creature and every plant has its life cycle.

Killing may help to fill my belly. But do I ever think about the animals that were relying on the one whose life I took?

You are sounding more like a philosopher than a wolf, I think.

I suppose I am. But I know one thing for certain: violence

took my son from me. And if there's any way for me to stop that from happening to another, then I believe I must try.

A wolf that does not kill. That is most definitely a new idea, my friend. Come, let's get some sleep. We need to make more progress tomorrow before the snow comes.

It was barely light outside when they heard the noise. At first, it was just a low, rumbling sound. But it soon grew louder and louder, echoing in the cave like the boom of thunder.

Ghost and Seti sleepily rose and stepped outside the cave.

Look!

Ghost indicated a rising plume of smoke that filled the sky. It seemed to be coming from the same place as the loud noise and it traveled across the horizon.

It can't be a fire – the smoke is moving too fast!

Seti smelled the air.

It's not a fire…it's more like the steam that comes out of the ground – the hot steam that can burn you if you get too close!

Without further discussion, they both started walking toward the source of the smoke and the noise. The ground rumbled beneath them as they got closer. Finally, they climbed a small hill and were met with an incredible sight that made them freeze in sheer amazement.

It was a steam engine pulling dozens of box cars along a rickety train track. The smoke from the stack billowed in great puffs, creating a cloud overhead that stretched backward for a mile.

The noise was overwhelming. Ghost and Seti stared at the monstrous thing with their mouths agape; they had never seen anything like it! After a few moments, the caboose appeared at the rear of the train and the massive locomotive turned the corner, chugging out of sight.

Ghost...what was that?

I don't know...but I hope I never see anything else like it.

Maybe...maybe this isn't such a good idea. I mean...there could be a lot of dangerous things like that out there, things we can't understand.

My father told me that the world is full of mysteries you can't understand unless you try.

I don't want to try to understand that thing. Ghost, if it ever tried to attack us, how could we stop it? I wouldn't even know where to start!

I don't think it's coming back, Seti. Besides, didn't you see the humans on it? Maybe it's like a wagon, but only bigger and faster.

You might be right. But all the same, let's be careful not to run into one of those things again!

By late afternoon, the two friends had reached the top of a mountain, giving them a broad view of the horizon. The sun was now behind them and toward the east, the sky was just beginning to darken into shades of crimson and purple.

Down below, they could make out a series of structures and they saw humans moving about. It was a small town, with a main street filled with shops and businesses and

scattered throughout the area, houses and barns.

Ghost, I'm hungry. We've been traveling all day and you've been eating grass, but there was nothing for me.

There are humans down there. We're sure to find food. Let's wait until it gets dark. We can't let anybody see us. Especially you!

They remained still, keeping a watchful eye for stray humans who might be coming their way. When the sun finally sank below the western horizon and twilight gave way to darkness, they moved slowly down the mountain, Seti leading the way with his expert night vision. They could see lights coming from within some of the buildings – candles burning brightly against the coal-black night.

I saw the humans leading horses into that barn. They must have food in there!

Seti, those are horses who have been working with their humans for years. They will be loyal to the ones who feed them and give them shelter. If I go into that barn, they'll be sure to alert the humans.

I'll never understand horses.

Seti closed his eyes and lifted his nose, sniffing.

There's food over there.

He indicated a row of buildings in the middle of town.

We can go behind, back there.

But quietly…

They approached the alley behind the row of shops. Most of the businesses were dark and quiet, but one of the buildings housed a saloon and it was filled with humans who were eating, drinking and making quite a bit of noise.

Ghost peered through a window.

What are they doing, Ghost?

Most of them are drinking something. And the more they drink, the louder they yell!

Seti leaped onto a wooden barrel and stared through the window.

Why are they doing that?

They must be thirsty, and then they yell because they're glad they're not thirsty anymore!

Seti noticed several crates on the ground near the rear door to the saloon.

Ghost, look! That's where the food is!

Seti leaped to the ground and raced to the crate. Inside was freshly cut meat, being kept outside in the cold to avoid spoilage. Seti pawed at the crate, which was nailed shut.

I can't get it open!

Ghost ambled to the crate and lifted a foreleg, bringing it down onto the wooden box. The top shattered, allowing Seti to pounce on the meat, which he did with extreme enjoyment. Ghost watched as Seti tore into his meal, taking enormous chunks of meat, filling his belly.

The sound of humans talking came from around the side of the building. Ghost tried to alert Seti.

Someone's coming!

But Seti was too absorbed in his feeding frenzy to hear Ghost. Ghost moved closer to Seti and tried to ease the crate of meat away from him. Instinctively, Seti growled and continued eating.

And then two humans appeared in the alley, their silhouettes lit from behind by the light from the window.

"A horse! Well, what's it doing out here in the dark?" The men walked closer to Ghost and then stopped in their tracks.

"Look out, that's a wolf!" The men ducked behind the wooden barrel and pulled out their weapons. Ghost recognized them from years earlier, when he had seen humans using their guns to kill horses.

Ghost reared up on his back legs and kicked at the men, neighing loudly. The wooden barrel fell over on its side and the men jumped out of the way, running back around the side of the building.

Ghost took advantage of their disappearance to run forward and kick the crate away from Seti, who was still gorging himself on the meat. Seti looked up, a snarl on his face.

What are you doing?!

Seti, the humans saw us! We have to leave!

Seti turned to run in the opposite direction but a human holding a gun appeared from the darkness, holding a weapon.

"I got him!" The human fired at Seti, just barely missing. The bullet struck the ground, kicking up a cloud of dust.

Ghost galloped toward the man, causing him to fall

backwards, dropping the gun. Seti started running behind Ghost, but just then, the man reached out and grabbed his pistol. Seti pivoted and ran in the other direction but heard men coming that way too.

Seti looked around and saw Ghost had managed to escape. With humans on both sides of him, he had no choice but to jump through the window.

Taking a few steps backward for momentum, Seti dug at the ground with his paws and, with a mighty effort, pushed off against the dirt and leaped into the air. He broke through the glass, shards falling all around him, and landed on his feet inside the saloon.

Patrons turned toward the direction of the breaking glass and saw Seti running at them. There were screams and shouts as humans fumbled to get out of the way of this attacking wolf! Seti looked around for a way out of the building, but there were too many people in the way. He jumped onto the long wooden bar, sending glasses and bottles flying! In a graceful arc, he jumped off of the bar, onto the top of a player piano, and then finally toward a staircase.

Now the men in the saloon were beginning to gather their wits. They rose slowly from their makeshift hiding places behind overturned tables and chairs, and with their guns drawn, headed for the staircase to chase after Seti.

Outside, Ghost had run as fast as he could to the outskirts of town. He thought that Seti was right behind him, but that turned out to be far from the truth. In fact, Seti was nowhere in sight! Ghost strained to listen for the sound of Seti running after him, but there was only the noise of humans yelling – and gunfire.

Ghost cautiously approached the front of the saloon, keeping an eye out for humans carrying weapons. He paused to peer into the saloon through a window and saw mass confusion – furniture and people scattered all about like kindling for a fire.

But there was no Seti! Where did he go? Was he lying somewhere, hurt?

Ghost's mind raced as he worried about his friend. But suddenly he heard the loud sound of glass breaking directly overhead. He moved further into the street so he could catch a glimpse of whatever was happening up there – and was stunned to see Seti racing across a balcony, being chased by humans who were shooting at him.

Ghost, run!

Without hesitation, Ghost galloped across the front of the saloon. Seti, full of determination and strength, leaped off of the balcony as bullets whizzed past his ears. He landed on Ghost's back and straddled the horse's neck with his four paws. Ghost never broke stride as the humans continued shooting at them.

Ghost ran into the darkness, where the humans couldn't see them. Seti jumped to the ground.

How was your meal, Seti?

Not good enough to make up for that!

They turned and continued running away from the town, along a road, with Seti guiding them through the darkness. They didn't stop until they were miles away.

Four

A cold wind blew across the shoreline, sending white-capped waves lapping against the tall ships moored in the harbor. Colorful flags atop the ship's masts flapped rapidly and seagulls beat their wings furiously, hovering overhead in search of fish swimming near the water's surface.

The largest vessel, a massive wooden ship with three masts and nearly one hundred men performing various tasks on her, was tied up at the main dock. Thick steel chains sunk into the water holding an anchor. There were two gangplanks – one leading to the ship's main deck, and one feeding into a hold. Dock workers pushed enormous crates up the plank, along with wooden barrels, sacks of flour and all types of parcels.

A steady stream of passengers lined up with their valises and trunks near the gang plank. There were families with small children, groups of sailors and, gathered near the stern, a colorful bunch of men, women and animals.

They were performers in a traveling circus, boarding the ship for Europe. Dock workers and roustabouts were struggling to push a reluctant donkey up the gang plank, trying to coax it with a carrot while heaving into its backside with all their strength. There were handfuls of acrobats and jugglers, whiling away the time by practicing their moves. Some sent pins flying through the air in intricate arcs, while others performed flips and cartwheels on the frozen cobblestone.

Finally, the donkey – either by agreement or sheer exhaustion – allowed itself to be guided up the gang plank. Now the roustabouts turned their attention to a much larger, and more worrisome, passenger.

They opened the rear gate of a wagon that had been parked near the dock. Reaching in to grab hold of several ropes, the men tugged gently but firmly, and soon a massive gray elephant emerged from the wagon. It lumbered down a wooden ramp, looked around at all the activity, then promptly let out a loud trumpeting call. Satisfied, it ambled down the stone pathway, onto the gangplank, and into the ship's hold.

Did you hear that?

Seti paused with his right front paw crooked, as if he was pointing at something up ahead.

It sounded like a horn – a loud one!

Ghost kept walking along the forest path and noticed a clearing just ahead.

Keep your eyes open for humans with weapons. They might be hunting.

The two friends exited the forest and found themselves atop a cliff that overlooked the ocean.

Seti – we made it! Look at that water!

I can't believe it! The ocean is so big!

It goes on forever!

Wait, be careful! There are humans down there!

Ghost looked down to where the ships were docked in the harbor. He gasped.

Those are the ships my father told me about! That's how the humans go from one country to another!

What, they climb onto those things? How do they stop them from sinking?

I don't know, but look at everything the humans are loading onto it! If it was going to sink, it would have been underwater by now.

Ghost, look down there – by the wagon. It looks like they're bringing horses right up to the top of that thing!

Ghost saw that Seti was telling the truth – roustabouts were guiding horses up the gang plank and herding them into stalls below deck.

Seti, we have to get down there! We've got to get onto that ship!

But how? We don't belong with them!

Down below, one of the humans held a long stick with a red ribbon tied at the end of it. He was waving it in front of a horse wearing an elaborate headdress and bridle. The horse was rearing up on its hind legs and holding its position.

Ghost, look at that horse! It's dancing for that human!

I've seen horses that were trained to carry humans but I've never seen anything like that!

There's another horse walking in circles!

Sure enough, a horse was being led by a human trainer to walk in a giant circle. When the human cracked a small whip in the air, the horse stopped and bowed low, touching its nose to the ground.

That's disgusting.

Seti was becoming upset at seeing the horses behave like that.

Ghost shook his head.

No, they're doing the job they were trained to do. And that gives me an idea about how to get on that boat. Listen...

Dock workers were carrying the last few packages up the ramp to the top deck. Several men lifted the ramp off the dock and carried it to a holding bin that led to the ship's control room. Overhead, steam shot out of a chimney as a loud, shrilling whistle blew signaling the ship was about to depart from the dock.

Ghost galloped down a cobblestone street and onto the dock area, just as workers were about to close the lower hatch, where the animals had been led. One of the human workers noticed Ghost.

"Wait a minute – there's another horse to be loaded!"

A man wearing a ship's uniform walked over to Ghost, checking some paperwork.

"There must be a mistake. We counted twelve circus horses. This one isn't part of the show."

The men proceeded to move toward the hatch, ready to close it. Ghost panicked. Remembering what the other circus horses had done, Ghost rose onto his rear legs and kicked his forelegs in the air while he neighed loudly. He stayed on his rear legs for a long time, dancing on the hard stone.

"Say, we could use a horse like that in the circus!" The man looked all around. "We'd better get him into the ship's hold before its owner comes and takes him away from us!"

Several dock workers guided Ghost toward the open hatch. Ghost looked around and spotted Seti hiding behind some wooden crates. He started neighing loudly, forcing everyone near the ship to turn and look at him.

Seti saw his opportunity! He ran as fast as he could and leaped onto the top deck of the ship before anyone could spot him. He looked all around for some place to hide – and saw a long wooden boat covered by a grey canvas. He struggled to force his body through a small opening, but it was too tight!

Just then, Seti heard footsteps coming. He bit at a rope that was holding the canvas on the boat. Using his powerful jaws, he chewed on the rope until he managed to fray and then tear it. With seconds to spare, Seti forced his body beneath the canvas. The humans walked past the boat, unaware of a wolf was hiding there.

Ghost took his place in a stall next to some of the circus horses. They looked at him with disgust.

What are you?

I…I don't know what you mean?

Look at yourself. Dirty. Uncombed. Look at your hooves. Filthy. Do you have any pride at all?

Ghost was taken aback by these words.

I'm a horse, just like you!

No, you are not! We are world famous performers. We travel by ship and train; we are groomed by the finest humans. We dance for kings. What do you do?

Well, I have a family…

That's all? A family? You mean you've created more dirty horses to run around in the mud?

The circus horses snickered. Ghost felt anger rising in his chest, but he took a few deep breaths and calmed himself. His father had taught him to never act in anger; if you wait a few moments and your anger subsides, then you can make a more logical decision.

You don't know me. You don't know my family. I suggest you control your desire to insult me. It will only lead to problems between us.

The circus horse snorted at Ghost and laughed.

Let's leave the family horse alone. Oh, but do let us know if you ever decide to become interesting, won't you?

Ghost couldn't believe how the horses were behaving. He had never known a horse to be so unwelcoming and unfriendly. He thought maybe this is what horses become when they are trained to seek approval from humans.

Ghost's thoughts turned to Seti. He saw Seti leap onto the ship and he didn't hear any humans crying out in panic at the sight of a wolf, so he was pretty sure Seti was safe. Still, it would be good to know for certain.

The ship set sail. Ghost could feel movement as the waves sent the ship up and down, and back and forth. Ghost's stomach rolled slightly at the motion – he had never experienced anything like this! But he didn't want the circus horses to notice his concern – they would only use it as an excuse to be cruel to him. He concentrated on thoughts of his family and did his best to avoid being seasick.

——⁓——

Seti was hungry. He had gone all that day and all that first night without food or drink. Hiding in the boat, he could hear humans moving around the deck, yelling loudly over the sound of crashing waves. The humans always seemed to be busy doing something – pulling ropes or making the ship emit loud noises. The one thing he did not see them do was eat a meal. Did humans need food? Or was that just animals?

When night fell again, Seti caught a scent of food, coming from inside one of the ship's many rooms. He pushed his snout through the opening between the canvas and the wooden boat, and inhaled deeply. His stomach

rumbled loudly with pangs of hunger. He kept a watchful
eye on the deck for a long time, waiting to see if any
humans were in the area. When he was certain there was
nobody around, he carefully moved out from beneath the
canvas and dropped to the ship's deck.

Seti's keen sense of smell and hunting instincts were
on full alert. He moved stealthily toward the source of the
scent; as he drew closer, he could hear humans talking
and laughing. He peered through a circular window and
saw many humans gathered around a long table, eating
and drinking.

Now Seti's stomach was aching! If he had been on land,
he could race into the room, snatch some food and make his
escape. But aboard the ship, there was no place for him to
hide. If the humans discovered a wolf in their midst, they
would surely kill him without a moment's hesitation.

Seti heard a door opening along the side of the ship.
Remaining close to the wall, in the darkness, he slowly crept
forward until he reached a large barrel with a wooden lid.
He could smell food coming from inside!

Seti stretched himself as tall as possible on his hind legs
and moved the lid with his nose. Inside the barrel were the
remains of half-eaten food – chicken legs, potatoes and
cornbread! Seti leaned in further to snatch some of the meat
in his jaws, but the barrel suddenly tipped over with a
clatter, sending its contents spilling all over the deck.

Seti heard the sound of human footsteps coming from

inside the ship. He took a few pieces of meat into his mouth and raced back to the boat. Behind him, he could hear a human yelling. At first, Seti thought he had been seen by the human, but as he made his way back to his hiding place, he realized the human was merely angry that the barrel of trash had toppled over.

Seti ate every bit of food he had brought with him as quickly as possible. His stomach full for the first time in more than a day, he settled against the wall and closed his eyes. He was asleep within seconds.

—◆—

Meanwhile, Ghost was roused from a standing sleep when a door opened and a human made his way down a rickety wooden staircase. The human was carrying a large sack, which he tossed to the ground with a thud. Pulling a knife from his pocket, he sliced a hole in the sack and then began filling several troughs in the circus horses' stalls. By the time the human reached Ghost, there was barely any food left. The human emptied the meager remains of the sack into Ghost's trough and walked away.

One of the circus horses noticed that Ghost had been given a smaller portion.

You see? Even the humans don't like you!

Ghost ignored the horse and began eating. The food was welcome – a mixture of grains and oats – and he didn't pause to catch his breath until all of it was gone.

Look at how he eats! Have you never been taught any manners, or were you raised with pigs?

Ghost gave the circus horse a dull look.

I was hungry. I haven't eaten in a day.

That's not our problem, mud horse. If you don't mind, try to behave with a little dignity, eh?

They were interrupted by the return of the human, who was carrying a plate of human food.

"Here you go, boy. There wasn't enough grain for you, so you can have some leftovers from upstairs."

The human dumped the contents of the plate into Ghost's trough – meat from the humans' meal. Savory and delicious, the food seemed a miracle to Ghost, who ate with even greater zeal than before. When he was finished, he looked up to see the circus horses staring at him with a mixture of hunger and jealousy in their eyes. Ghost chuckled.

I guess he likes mud horses better than circus horses.

The circus horses snorted their disapproval and turned to face the other direction, snubbing Ghost for the rest of the night.

―⁓―

Seti woke with a start. His body was being slammed back and forth in the bottom of the wooden boat. At first, he thought a human was battering him – but when his vision finally adjusted to the dark, he realized the large ship itself was rocking violently. Every time Seti tried to lift himself to an upright position, the ship would sway and he would be tossed backward again.

He could hear the humans on the ship rushing about frantically; their cries were loud and full of emotion and it struck Seti that this kind of situation was not something that happened often. If it had, the humans would be more in control of themselves. Instead, they sounded panicked and frightened for their lives.

Below, in the hold, the circus animals were also being battered by the violent motion of the ship. The circus horses were neighing loudly, their eyes wide with fear. Ghost, however, was working hard to remain calm. He breathed in and out carefully, as his father had taught him to do in dangerous situations. That way, his mind would not give way to the same terror the other horses were suffering from.

Ghost widened his stance so he wouldn't be knocked off his legs by the severe sway of the ship. Many of the other horses had already fallen, and one of them appeared to have broken a leg. Ghost knew how terrible that was for a horse – a broken leg could spell the end of its ability to walk, let alone perform. Worse, it might give humans cause to end its life.

The circus horse that had been insulting Ghost the day before was panicking in its stall.

What's happening? Why won't our humans come to save us?

Ghost moved close to the other horse and pressed

against it, helping to keep it upright.

They are probably having the same kind of trouble as we are. Try to focus on staying upright. Breathe deeply and do not allow your fear to swallow you.

How can I help it? We're all going to die!

We won't. This is only a storm. It won't last for long and when it's over, we'll still be here.

The circus horse calmed slightly, nodding quietly. It was still afraid, but Ghost had reassured it enough so it could endure what was happening.

"Man overboard!"

Seti heard the cry from underneath the canvas. He heard more loud yelling and footsteps skidding on the wet surface of the deck.

"Get the lifeboat!"

Suddenly, Seti could tell there were humans just outside the boat he was hiding in. They were trying to undo the ropes that held the canvas snugly onto the boat, but the rope was wet, and the men couldn't undo the knots.

"We need a knife!"

The humans continued working the ropes and managed to untie several knots, lifting the canvas slightly. Torrents of rain poured into the boat as Seti hugged the rear wall, trying to remain hidden. A human arrived and began cutting at the rope, hacking the knots away so the canvas could be lifted.

And then it happened. An enormous wave crashed into

the ship, sending it nearly sideways! The humans were sent skittering across the deck like rag dolls, smashing into pipes and debris and each other, helpless and unable to grab onto anything.

As far as the ship had tilted one way, it now tilted the other and now the humans were sent rolling back toward Seti and the wooden boat.

"Get below or we're drowned for sure!" A voice cried out to the humans and they all took advantage of the slight pause in the ship's movement to fight their way to the door leading to the ship's hold.

Seti was safe, but only from the humans. Now he was in a lifeboat that was nearly halfway full of water. Even with the rocking motion of the boat causing some of the water to splash out, he knew it would only be a matter of time before the boat filled with water over his head.

Seti scrambled out of the boat and found himself in the middle of a massive downpour of rain. He looked around the deck for another boat to hide in, but there were none in the area. He raced up a flight of stairs leading to the captain's deck. There was a place inside, safe from the rain, but the door was closed, and there was no way to get in.

Seti noticed something moving in the water; it was a human, fighting to remain above the water line. The man was utterly frightened, his eyes wide and he was gasping for air. Every time he managed to stay above water for a few seconds, another massive wave rolled over him.

Seti had no affection whatsoever for humans – he had heard far too many stories of their cruelty to wolves. He had been taught and he felt by instinct, that they were never to be trusted.

And yet, as Seti watched the man helplessly flailing in the water, he felt compassion. What if the human had a family? Young ones to care for?

With the wind and rain lashing at him, Seti fought to remain on his feet as he maneuvered himself toward the rear of the ship. With a closer view, he could now see the human was trying to reach a white circular object that had been tossed to him by another human. Seti guessed it was something that would help the man stay afloat. He watched as the human fought, time after time, to reach the round object. But it was clear the human was losing the battle. He was moving his arms less quickly, and his gasps for air came louder and longer. Seti knew the human would be dead within seconds.

Without thinking, Seti dove into the churning waters. Initially stung by the cold temperature, Seti quickly began paddling, which helped to warm his body. He now felt the full impact of the waves, as they crashed, one after another, sending him spinning and twisting in the water.

Finally, Seti reached the circular object. There was a rope attached to it, and Seti bit down hard to make sure he wouldn't lose it in the swirling waters. He started swimming to the human, who was no longer flailing his arms, too tired to continue his attempts to remain afloat. The man was starting to sink into the water.

Seti reached the human, who barely had enough energy left to see the wolf coming toward him. Exhausted and freezing, the human slipped his arm through the life preserver, and allowed Seti to guide him back toward the ship. The waves began pushing Seti and the human away from the ship. Seti realized he had to swim at an angle in order to avoid being hopelessly lost in the cold waters.

A giant wave pushed against the ship from the side opposite where Seti and the human were. The great ship listed toward Seti and looked as if it would capsize. But somehow, the ship righted itself. Seti only had to swim a few yards more toward the ship and was able to stand on a step jutting off the ship's side. The human was still holding onto the life preserver, but he was nearly unconscious. His head bobbed helplessly as the water lapped around him.

Overhead, the sky lightened a bit and a strong wind carried more storm clouds away. With the rain stopping, Seti shook his fur, releasing most of the water from his body. He kept his eye on the human, fearing he might panic at the sight of a wolf, as humans tend to do.

"Down here! He's down here!" A voice cried from the top deck of the ship. Seti turned to look up and saw a group of humans, all waving and shouting, pointing in his direction. A rope ladder was tossed over the side of the ship, and several humans began climbing down.

"What in the world…?" The first human to reach Seti's location stared at him with surprise. "It looks like a wolf!"

"That's exactly what it is!" Another human arrived and reached down to pull the unconscious human out of the water. Both men tugged with all their might; the man was heavy, and the water made it even more difficult to hold him. Once they had the man onto the step safely, they turned their attention to Seti.

"We can't have a wolf on the ship – not with those circus animals at his mercy."

"Push him off and let's get back up on deck," said the second man.

But just as the men were about to kick Seti back into the water, the injured man opened his eyes and grunted loudly.

"No! It saved me…" The man could barely keep his eyes open, but there was an emotional urgency to his voice. "The wolf…saved my life…"

The other two men stared at each other in disbelief.

"He must be delirious," said the first man.

"But what if he isn't? I mean, wolves are pretty smart."

The two men secured a harness around the injured man and gave the signal for their shipmates to haul him up to the deck.

"Take him up!" The men on the top deck began hauling the injured man up, working in unison to bring him higher and higher until he was safe.

The two men stared at Seti.

"I'm not going to pick him up."

"I'll do it. But if he bites me, he's going in the drink."

The man leaned down and slid his arms beneath Seti.
Seti was on guard – he had never been this close to a human
before and his wolf instincts were alerted. But he remained
calm, allowing the human to lift him. Every instinct in his
body kept him vigilant, just in case. But for the first time in
his life, he surrendered and allowed another creature to
control his fate.

Seti was carried onto the deck and into a small cabin,
where the humans arranged a blanket on the floor for him
to lie down. They brought a ceramic bowl and filled it with
fresh water, which he drank thirstily and brought him a ham
bone. Seti's normal instinct was to protect his food by
growling at any other creatures in the area, but he somehow
realized the humans would not try to take the bone away
from him. He chewed on it with focused attention,
delighting in the flavor and the fullness of his stomach.

Later, after Seti had sated his appetite, the humans left
him alone in the cabin. He fell asleep, his mind and body
completely exhausted. The ship's now-gentle rocking
propelled him into a deep slumber that lasted all that day
and into the next morning.

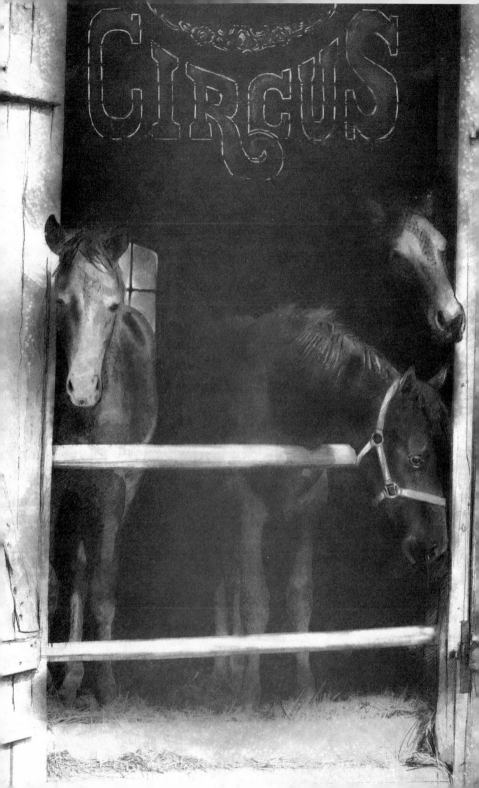

In the hold, Ghost and the circus horses were back in their respective stalls after the humans had cleared away the mess of water and waste that had splashed everywhere during the storm.

The humans had come to Ghost's stall and placed a colorful bridle on him; with no place to run, Ghost remained calm. It would have done him no good to fight as long as the humans could keep him pinned in the stall.

When the humans left, the circus horse next to Ghost spoke up.

They're going to bring you into the circus.

What does that mean?

It means you will be just like us – performing tricks, traveling around the world. It's not a bad life, really. As long as you let them train you, they'll treat you fairly.

But I don't want to be in the circus! We – I mean – I'm on a journey to trace the paths of my ancestors. I must reach the castle where they were the most glorious horses in all of history!

The circus horse gave Ghost a skeptical look.

Well, I don't know about all of that. But it sounds to me like you're asking for nothing but misery. The circus is a good home! Look, I know I was mean to you before and I apologize for that. Come on and become a circus horse. I'll teach you how to get by without any trouble. I'm sure you could learn to do the tricks. Here, I'll show you one. When the human comes and snaps the whip once, it means we're supposed to bend forward, like this!

The circus horse leaned his head down and crooked a foreleg. It looked as if he was bowing.

Can you do it?

Ghost felt a little silly, but he imitated the movement of the horse perfectly.

Like that?

Exactly!

But why do they need to use a whip? Do they hit you with it?

Only if you won't do the trick!

Have you ever been hit with a whip?

Once or twice...it doesn't really hurt.

Are you sure about that?

The circus horse quickly changed the subject.

That doesn't matter! What's important is that we have good homes, good food, friendship – and we have all that in exchange for performing a few tricks.

I don't want to insult you, but I believe I'd rather have my freedom.

The circus horse stared at Ghost. There was a softening

in his eyes and a kind of sadness. It seemed to Ghost the circus horse might be thinking about that word – freedom.

———

For the next few days, the seas were calm. Seti had grown accustomed to sleeping in the cabin where the humans had brought him. And the human he had saved, Taylor, had taken a special interest in him. Taylor spent a great deal of time with Seti – at first cautiously, but then as time went by, a bit more familiarly. Taylor brought small treats for Seti from the ship's kitchen – bits of meat, and of course, bones. Seti instinctively knew that Taylor had no bad intentions. For the first time, Seti found himself trusting a human.

"You're my hero, you are," said Taylor. Seti allowed himself to be gently petted on the head by the man. "I'll never know where you came from or how you found me, but you saved me, all right."

Taylor would take Seti onto the deck when the ocean was fairly smooth. They would watch great fish swimming, with their sharp-angled fins protruding from the water. And once, in the distance, a whale appeared, spouting a tremendous fountain of water into the air.

The one thing Seti would not do – could not make himself do – was to perform little tricks in exchange for food. Taylor attempted to teach Seti how to shake hands and sit and Seti was fully aware of what the human wanted from him.

But Seti's pride as a wolf prevented him from even considering such foolishness. He was a pack leader, a father and grandfather. Despite his positive feelings for Taylor, Seti would not allow his animal nature to be tainted.

—*ᴡᴡ*—

One day, the circus humans came to the hold with a lot of equipment they had not brought with them before. There were brushes and clippers – and a box of colorful, shiny things that Ghost couldn't understand. The humans began grooming the circus horses, smoothing their manes and trimming their tails. Ghost was amazed at how calmly the horses were accepting it all; the humans were turning them into versions of themselves that were very different from the horses they actually were.

One of the humans approached Ghost and began examining him.

"This one needs a lot of work," he said. "We'll have to clip those hooves, and this mane is all knots. Come on, with three of us at once, we can work faster."

The humans moved closer to Ghost and started using their tools on him, but Ghost bucked and neighed loudly. Once again, the men tried to brush Ghost's hair, but he resisted.

You'd better let them do it.

Ghost looked up and saw that the circus horse was speaking to him.

They won't leave you alone until it's done. And what's the big deal? So they comb your hair. It doesn't hurt.

They'll make me look ridiculous!

They've been feeding you. They think you belong to them.

I don't!

Really? Then why don't you walk out of this place and swim home?

Ghost exhaled, slightly angry the horse was correct. He turned to the humans and lowered his head.

"He's calmed down," one of the humans said. "Let's get the job finished before he kicks one of us!"

The humans busily moved across Ghost's body, snipping here, brushing there. When they were finished, they fastened a decoration on his head – a shiny red piece of metal and fabric that had a tall red feather on top.

"All right, this one's done. Let's go topside and get those banners ready."

The humans exited up the staircase. Ghost tried to look up and see what was on his head, but it was impossible. The circus horses turned to admire Ghost.

Ooh, the red one, that's my favorite. You're lucky, it's not as heavy as the others, but it's the one that sparkles the most under the bright lights.

What are you talking about?

When we're in the center ring of the circus for the parade, there are spotlights that shine down on us so the people can see us better. And your headdress looks wonderful in those lights.

But I'm not going to —

Ghost couldn't complete his sentence because at that moment, the hatch door opened, spilling bright sunlight into the ship's hold for the first time in a week. Ghost blinked his eyes rapidly, trying to adjust to the sudden light. The next thing he knew, a human was placing a rope around his neck and leading him out of his stall, through the hatch and down a wooden plank. The rest of the horses were also led behind Ghost. They proceeded in a straight line down a long wooden dock, where there were dozens of humans rushing around, unloading items from the ship.

Ghost could hear loud music coming from the distance. He looked up and saw hundreds of humans waiting behind a rope line. They were clapping and cheering, and Ghost was confused about what they were looking at.

Lift your head up! Walk proudly!

The circus horse behind Ghost called out to him and the other horses.

What are those humans doing? Why are they yelling?

They're here to see us! Humans love seeing animals!

But why?

Because we do tricks. Watch!

The circus horse reared onto its hind legs and pranced, kicking his forelegs out in front of him rhythmically. The humans let out a loud cheer. Small children had big smiles

on their faces. Ghost still couldn't understand it all.

I knew humans were strange, but this is worse than I thought.

On the deck, Taylor led Seti out of the cabin and kneeled down next to him.

"You're gonna like living in my house, you are," said the man to Seti. "The missus and the kids, well, they'll treat ya like one of the family for sure."

With that, Taylor slipped a collar around Seti's neck, attacked to a leash.

"All's I gotta do is get my rucksack from my quarters and we'll be on our way. Come on, hup!"

The man tried to lead Seti down the gang plank, but the wolf pulled away. He didn't like having the collar around his neck.

"Whoa then! I know how you feel, boy, but I can't let you run wild in town. These folks'll be scared enough as it is, seeing a wolf in their midst. But as long as I've got ya tied, why, there's nothin' they can say about it, am I right? Let's go, boy. I don't want to have to carry ya!"

Seti grudgingly allowed himself to be led down the gang plank. As humans walked past him, many recoiled at the sight of a wolf. But Seti did his best to avoid making eye contact with them. He walked with his head down, alongside Taylor, with an eye toward making his escape as soon as possible.

Taylor tied his leash to a post.

"I won't be five minutes, boy! Stay here and don't be a nuisance barkin' at the kiddos, eh?"

Taylor gave Seti a pat on the head and hustled back up the gang plank in search of his belongings. Seti lowered himself to the ground and laid his head in between his two front paws. He kept a wary eye out for misbehaving humans, as he still believed they were capable of cruelty at any moment.

He wondered where Ghost was. The last time he saw his friend, he was being escorted into the bottom of the great ship. Did Ghost survive the journey?

At that moment, Seti heard a loud cheer coming from a place that was beyond his line of vision. Obviously, the humans were all gathered together for some reason – what could it be?

Ghost followed the humans who were leading the horses toward a freight car on the railroad tracks. The car had iron bars in the windows, and there were already animals in some of the other cars – and the door was closed securely. The horses inside the cars looked through the small windows; they had gone from being held in the bottom of the ship to being held in the railroad cars.

Ghost panicked. If he set foot inside one of those cars, he would never be able to find Seti! And even worse, he wouldn't be able to find the castle his ancestors had served. The entire journey would be for nothing!

Ghost suddenly had an idea. Keeping an eye on the

humans, Ghost reared up on his hind legs and started prancing. Suddenly, the humans turned toward him and started clapping and yelling for him.

"Here, stop that!" One of the circus humans tried to force Ghost back to the ground and into the train car.

But Ghost wouldn't stop prancing. He neighed loudly and leaped into the air, kicking his hind legs up, and then nodding his head, tossing his mane. Every new move he made gave the humans even more to cheer for. He stepped sideways, he pivoted and knelt down – and the audience nearly swooned with appreciation for the show they were being treated to!

The humans were reluctant to stop Ghost because he was creating tremendous good will – which meant more people would come to see the circus. They all acted as if Ghost's behavior was part of the plan, and they took deep bows in front of the audience, smiling and hoping that Ghost would stop his antics soon.

Ghost scampered onto a push cart, then leaped to a staircase that led to the street above. The audience delighted in Ghost's antics – much to the dismay of the circus workers who were attempting to herd the horses into the train car.

From Ghost's vantage point, high above the crowd, he could see the entire ship that had carried him across the ocean. He scanned the area, but couldn't see Seti anywhere. And then he heard a familiar sound.

Beyond the clatter of people, workers, ship whistles and

the crashing ocean waves, Ghost could hear the clear, pure sound of a wolf's cry. His eyes followed the sound, and he looked at the far end of the ship, near the gang plank.

Seti! He was tied to a post, standing on his hind legs, howling as loudly as possible!

Ghost jumped off of the staircase, directly over the heads of the humans who were gathered to watch him perform. Believing this to be part of the circus, the audience clapped loudly and cheered for Ghost.

But Ghost only had one thing in mind – to reach Seti before the humans could grab him! He landed onto the cobblestone road, which made for unsteady running. But he somehow managed to remain on his feet, as he dodged workers carrying trunks and barrels and suitcases. As he galloped past the humans, he saw them dash madly out of his path, their eyes wide with fear, tossing packages into the air and scrambling to get away!

Finally, Ghost reached Seti.

You made it!

What's that thing on your head?

Never mind!

It makes you look silly!

I said never mind! Who tied you here?

It's a long story – but he's coming back, so we'd better get away!

I'll try to bite through this…

Ghost bit down hard on the leather leash that was tied

to the wooden post.

"Hey, what are you doing!?" Ghost and Seti looked up to see Taylor, the human who had befriended Seti, on the deck of the ship, holding his belongings.

Hurry Ghost! He's coming!

Ghost worked his teeth on the leather strap, grinding them back and forth like a knife. He was making progress, but not fast enough. And now he heard Taylor's footsteps coming toward them!

Ghost panicked. He turned to face Taylor and neighed loudly, keeping him at bay. With his back to Seti, Ghost kicked at the wooden post, snapping it in two!

You did it, Ghost! Come on!

Ghost turned and raced along the shoreline. Seti followed closely, with half of the wooden post dangling from the leash around his neck. It pulled terribly – and every time the post clattered onto the ground, Seti felt a tight, painful jerk on his neck. He started lagging behind Ghost, becoming weary with the effort of pulling the post along behind him.

I…I can't make it, Ghost!

Ghost stopped and looked behind him. Seti was indeed slowing down – with the human, and the circus workers running after them! Ghost looked ahead and saw something that gave him an idea.

Don't give up yet! This way!

Ghost raced up a hill to where some shops and

businesses indicated the outskirts of a small town. Between the town and the waterfront, however, was a train track – and in the distance, Ghost could see puffs of smoke from an oncoming train.

Seti reached his side, breathless from the effort of running.

Seti, come on, we'll stand on the other side – with the wooden post here!

What do you mean?

Let that thing around your neck lay here. When that train comes, it'll run right across it and you'll be free!

But…I don't want to be that close to…whatever that is!

Behind them, the humans were nearly to the top of the hill. The train was coming closer and closer.

If we don't go now, we'll never make it! You have to trust me!

Seti looked from the humans to the train to Ghost.

Okay…

At the very last possible moment, Ghost and Seti leaped across the train track, leaving the wooden post on the ground behind them. The leather leash stretched across the track – just barely. Seti had to lean forward, nearly in the path of the oncoming train.

The humans arrived just as the train did. The engine and the remaining cars whirred past in a blur. When the last car finally went past, the humans were stunned to see that Ghost and Seti were gone. All that was left was the remains of the leather leash, and the wooden post, lying at their feet.

———

I don't see a castle.

Seti walked alongside Ghost as they made their way down a country road. They had been walking for two days, and Seti was beginning to feel that the story about castles might not be true after all.

I know it's here somewhere, Seti! My father would never have lied about that!

I'm sure he wasn't lying, but maybe somebody else told him a lie. Maybe it was just somebody telling him a story when he was little, you know, like a bedtime story?

No, it had to be true. There were so many details – how the castle sits atop a mountain, and from a distance, it looks like someone had carved it right out of the mountain itself!

Well…how long do you think we'll need to keep walking before we get there? I mean, it's really getting cold now. What if it snows?

But as long as we keep going in the direction of the sunrise, we're sure to get there soon.

Ghost, look! Horses!

Up ahead, penned by a wooden fence, were several horses grazing on the meager grass that remained on the ground. Ghost turned to Seti.

Stay here, I'll go talk to them.

Ghost cantered up the road where the horses had turned to watch the approach of this stranger. He casually moved closer to the fence, not wanting to alarm them.

Hello! I was wondering if one of you might know where the castle is!

Go away! We don't need trouble from outsiders!

I…I'm not trying to cause any trouble…but I've come a very long way, and I really need to reach –

One of the horses took a menacing step forward.

What do you want with the castle?

Nothing…

Then why go? There's nothing there for you! There's nothing left!

Ghost stared at the horse, suddenly struck with a horrible feeling of panic.

What…what do you mean?

The war took care of that. Stupid humans…

War? I didn't know about a war…

Castle was there for hundreds of years. Humans don't even protect the things they build themselves.

Ghost's breath came faster as his mind raced. How could he tell Seti the castle had been destroyed, after they had come so far?

My ancestors lived there. They carried soldiers into battle for generations…

Huh? I think you must be mistaken about that. There were no soldiers at that castle. Not until the ones who came and destroyed it.

I…I don't understand! My father told me…

Go see for yourself. It's two day's walk, straight ahead.

Ghost was numb. He could barely think straight. He turned to the horses.

Well…thank you for letting me know.

Too bad what those humans do!

Ghost walked slowly back to where Seti had been hiding behind some tall trees.

What did they say, Ghost?

Well…they told me the castle is two days' walk from here, but…

Two days? That's wonderful! Let's get started!

Seti, I need to tell you –

Tell me on the way!

With that, Seti raced down the road toward the castle. Within seconds, he was just a dot on the horizon. Ghost exhaled deeply and began running after him.

The landscape changed from mostly farmland and meadows to rocky fields and then deep forest. Ghost caught up to Seti, who was waiting for him near the outer stand of trees.

I guess we keep going straight through the forest, right Ghost?

Ghost looked left and right, noticing the trees extended in both directions as far as the eye could see.

We won't be able to go very fast – there's no trail.

That never stopped us before, did it? Come on!

Seti plunged into the forest, skidding around the trees with the energy and enthusiasm of a young pup. Ghost followed, but it was more difficult for him to navigate past the trees. He kept his eyes in the direction where Seti had run, for fear of losing his traveling companion. He knew that when Seti was in a hurry, there was no way of slowing him down.

It was true – Seti was already a half-mile into the forest. Every now and then, he'd stop to sniff the air so he could catch Ghost's scent. What was taking him so long?

Seti noticed the forest was becoming darker and darker. There were more tall fir trees, with thicker boughs, overhead. They blocked out the sun more dramatically than the other trees had and soon it felt as though Seti was traveling in the middle of the night.

As he moved cautiously forward, he began smelling something unusual – it was a dark, pungent odor, one he hadn't ever smelled before. It grew stronger, and he was curious enough to follow it.

As Seti came into a small clearing, he saw piles of bones scattered on the ground. He approached them cautiously; he was on high alert for any animal predators that may be in the area.

When he reached the bones, he immediately realized they weren't animal bones – they were human. He could tell by the size and shape of the skulls, some of which had large holes in them.

Lying next to some of the bones were long wooden things – and Seti recognized them as the tools the humans used to kill one another. They made loud noises and sent something flying from the tool directly into the bodies of their enemies. Sometimes those tools were used on animals, too.

Ghost finally reached the clearing, and saw what Seti was looking at.

Something bad happened here, Ghost.

Seti…those horses back there…they told me that there was a war in this area, not too long ago…

Then these humans must have been part of it. Look, these are what they use to kill each other.

Yes…and they said something else…

But before Ghost could finish his sentence, they both heard the snap of a branch, further in the forest, where it was too dark to see.

Did you hear that, Ghost?

Yes…there's something out there…

Then came another snapping noise, this time from a different direction.

A human slowly emerged from the deep forest. He was moving slowly, as if he was in pain. His clothes were torn and ragged, and his bones seemed to stick out from beneath his skin, making him look only slightly healthier than those dead soldiers on the ground.

Another human, equally gaunt, with haunted eyes and one arm missing, limped out of the darkness. He was propped up under one arm by a crude crutch, and in the other hand he held a sharpened stick.

"There's a meal, sure as I live," he said.

"Careful though," said the other. "One jab in the neck'll do the job…"

Seti let out a low growl.

Ghost, I…I made a vow to never use violence again…

Maybe we should just run…

As Ghost spoke, another human, this one covered in caked blood, his clothes all but fallen off of his thin frame, emerged from another direction.

"The way I see it, we kill the wolf first, the horse can't run too quick through these trees," said the first man. "Once we get the wolf down, I'm claimin' his fur as a coat. You lot can have the rest."

"Oh, I ain't had steak in nearly a year," said the second man, moving forward toward Ghost. "This creature'll feed us for a week."

One of the men leaped at Seti, but the wolf moved sideways quickly, causing the man to fall to the ground. Another man grabbed at Seti's tail and hung on as Seti twisted and spun around, trying to loosen the man's grip.

The third man lunged at Ghost and buried his sharpened stick several inches into Ghost's neck. Ghost neighed in pain and shook his body furiously, then spun his whole body around and kicked at the man. One of Ghost's hooves caught the man in the chest, sending him flying backward into a tree. The man was stunned. He dropped the stick and his eyes rolled back into his head. Ghost quickly moved forward and stepped on the stick, breaking it into pieces.

By now, both of the other men were grabbing at Seti, who growled and snapped, but wouldn't bite them. There were many opportunities for him to do so, but Seti instead chose to try and twist his body away from their clutches.

Seti, defend yourself!

Ghost couldn't bear to see his friend being mauled! He stepped forward and head-butted one of the men, sending him crashing to the ground. Ghost reared back on his hind legs and towered over the man, ready to stomp on him.

Ghost, don't do it! No more violence!

Ghost couldn't believe his ears – the humans were trying to kill them, but Seti refused to meet their attack with equal force. Ghost moved away from the human and stood watching Seti struggling to free himself from the third man's grasp. The human was losing energy quickly – it was obvious that he was tired and hungry, probably starving. Despite his intentions, the human simply didn't have the strength to take down a mature wolf.

Finally, the human succumbed to his fatigue and, breathing heavily, fell to the ground. Seti, also breathless, stepped away from him and stood next to Ghost. He looked up at his friend, who had blood pouring down his neck.

Ghost, are you all right?

It hurts, but I'll be okay. Let's get away from these humans, before they get their strength back.

Ghost and Seti continued moving through the thick

stand of trees. They had survived yet another near-disaster, and Ghost was wondering if he had made the biggest mistake of his life by coming all this way and bringing Seti along.

That night, the wind turned even colder and a light, freezing rain fell from the sky. It created a soft, tinkling sound as the tiny ice particles hit the branches overhead. Ghost and Seti huddled together for warmth and comfort, though they found little of either. They were lost in a foreign land, with predators and potential enemies in every direction. Having been told the castle had been destroyed, Ghost now felt as if he had betrayed Seti's trust and, even worse, his friendship.

He decided to continue on the next day to the castle, and allow events to run their course. He knew the moment would bring sadness into his heart and he hoped that Seti wouldn't turn against him in anger for having brought him so far for so little. As Seti snored softly, Ghost found himself unable to sleep. He gave up trying and simply kept watch. He couldn't ever remember feeling worse.

When the sun finally rose, Ghost stood and stamped his feet, shivering from the cold. Billowing clouds formed when he exhaled and there was frost on the ground.

Seti stirred, opening his eyes.

Today is your big day, Ghost. You'll finally see that castle.

Yes...

I'm happy for you. Despite how hard it has been, I'm glad to have made the journey with you.

At that moment, they noticed snow was beginning to fall.

We'd better get going, Ghost. I want to reach that castle before the snow slows us down. Hopefully we'll find some food on the way.

So they began their morning's journey. It took only a short while before they reached the edge of the forest, and began traveling through a hilly area with many slopes and small valleys. There were meager berry bushes that hadn't fully died in the change of seasons that gave both of them some much-needed nourishment. And in the lower valleys, they found small, standing bodies of water where they could drink to their fill.

Also strewn about the ground was more evidence of the war that had been fought by humans in the area. Burnt wagons, scattered bones, and many metal and wooden items that Ghost and Seti recognized as human weapons. The fighting must have spread over many miles. Ghost wondered what could have provoked the humans to cause them to waste their own lives, and the lives of their fellow humans.

As they proceeded toward the sunrise, they could see an outline of some kind of structure in the distance. It was in the middle of a stark and grassless plain, and it appeared to be made from large blocks of cut stone.

Ghost, is that the castle?

Ghost looked in the distance and saw the structure. Without words, he began galloping toward it, paying no attention to the rocky, uneven ground beneath his hooves.

When he came within a hundred yards of the structure, he saw that it was, in fact, a castle – one that had been burned and destroyed, with great piles of broken stones scattered all around it.

Ghost walked slowly towards the ruins. He could immediately see the castle hadn't been very large to begin with....But his father had described an immense castle that sat on top of a mountain! This one was situated on a plain – and it could hardly be called immense!

Ghost felt his heart leap in his chest. This wasn't the castle that his father had spoken about, not in the least!

Seti, it's the wrong castle! Isn't that great?

Seti approached Ghost cautiously, watching Ghost's excitement with curiosity.

I don't know, Ghost...is it great?

Ghost pranced and leaped in the air.

Yes! Oh Seti, I was so afraid that my father's castle was destroyed!

Why would you think that?

Because those horses back there –

Suddenly he stopped, realizing that he had kept what the horses had said to him private, and hadn't shared it with Seti.

Um…I have a confession to make, Seti. Those horses told me that this castle was ruined in the war, and I thought it was the castle my father told me about. I didn't tell you because I was afraid you wouldn't want to keep going on our journey. I thought if you knew the castle was destroyed, you might have turned around and gone back home…

Ghost, even if your father's castle was set on fire; if it was made of mud; if there turns out to be no castle at all, I would never leave you on your own. I promised you I'd come with you on this adventure. I'd never break my word to you.

I'm sorry, Seti. I should have trusted you. I should have trusted your friendship.

Yes, you should have. But I'm afraid this means we still don't know where your father's castle is.

All we can do is keep going in the same direction, I guess. Toward sunrise.

Seti looked up at the sky. It was slate-grey, and the snow was falling steadily now. The ground was beginning to turn white.

The snow is really coming down now, Ghost. Let's keep moving, it'll keep us warm.

As they continued walking past the remains of the castle, Ghost felt relief. He had finally told Seti the truth, and Seti wasn't angry with him for withholding it. Ghost's father had told him – and it had been proven true many times – that telling the truth was the best way to walk through life. It was the least we owed to each other as fellow creatures.

As they continued walking toward the sunrise, they would occasionally pass near small villages, where they had to be very careful to avoid being seen by humans. They had learned their lesson to never step foot in a village unless it was absolutely necessary.

But finding food in the wintertime was increasingly difficult; they could forage in areas where the snow hadn't yet fallen, but even the large farm fields yielded little worth eating.

They were also faced with the daunting task of crossing a number of rivers – something made more difficult by the fact that the water was so cold at this time of year. Many of the rivers had bridges that Seti and Ghost could cross, as long as there were no humans watching them. But most of them were in the middle of the countryside, and had to be crossed at a narrow point, if one could be found, or by swimming.

When they were forced to swim to the other side of the rivers, they faced an even greater hardship because their fur and coat remained wet in the freezing air, and sometimes even froze solid. The crossings exhausted them, but they had to keep moving so their bodies would generate heat. All in all, the rivers were the least pleasant sight during their journey.

The weather had now turned so cold that the snow on the ground wouldn't melt. In fact, in many places, the snow had frozen into ice, which made it harder for Ghost to walk. Seti would run ahead and scout paths where the snow wasn't quite so solid. It meant their progress was slowing; they had to fight for each bit of forward movement.

Relief came in the form of a city – the largest that either of them had ever seen. It was set at the base of two large rivers, and several steamships were anchored at a port there. Ghost and Seti recognized the bustle of activity, with dozens of humans loading and unloading barrels and crates from ships to waiting wagons.

From high above a mountain, Ghost and Seti looked down on the city, filled with awe. They could see hundreds, maybe even thousands, of people moving about in wagons and on busy streets. There were smaller versions of the train they had seen earlier – metal boxes with wheels that carried one or two people, and the boxes moved quickly down the streets, occasionally producing a honking horn sound!

Ghost, there must be food down there – and I'm really hungry!

Remember what happened last time we got too close to the humans, Seti. I'm not sure we could get away again.

If we wait until night time…

I don't think it's a good idea…

But we'll starve if we don't find food!

Wait – look down there! It's a horse pulling a wagon! I'll ask him where we can find a meal!

If he's pulling a wagon, that means he's got a human with him.

No – the human just jumped off the wagon! He's unloading

something and carrying it into that building! I'm going before he comes back!

Ghost – wait –

But Ghost was already racing down a path on the mountainside. He approached the horse that was attached to the wagon by two long poles on either side, and a bridle with long straps.

Hello! Say, I was wondering if you could tell me where I might find some food?

The horse looked alarmed when he spotted Ghost.

You can't be on the loose like that! Where's your master?

I…I don't have a master…

Then somebody will surely capture you! Horses aren't allowed to wander free here!

What should I do?

My master is delivering milk to his customers – wait in the hills, just over there and then follow the wagon back to our farm. When the master puts me up for the night in the barn, I can let you eat something. If you like oats and apples…

I do! Oh, thank you! Thank you so much…Um…I should tell you, I have a friend who is also very hungry…

We do not have the means to feed very many horses…

He's not a horse…

You travel with another kind?

Yes…we grew up together…and we are great friends…

What type of beast?

Well, he's…sort of a dog…

Oh well, a dog – they eat scraps, that will present no problem. So long as he stays away from the chickens. And don't let the master see him! For the master has many cats in his house, they are his children. No dog will ever cross his threshold and live to tell the tale!

I'll let him know. Thank you.

Ahh, but a word of warning – one of the other horses on the farm, his name is Odessa, he will not welcome you, nor your friend. In fact, he will be most unwelcoming – even going so far as to try and harm you! Stay clear of him! Look! My master comes – you must go!

Ghost scampered away quickly, hiding behind another wagon that had been left a short distance away. The rear door to a building opened, and a human stepped out carrying an empty milk container. He loaded it into the back of the wagon and climbed up. He flicked the leather reins and the horse began moving up the road leading out of town.

When they had passed, Ghost quickly galloped up the mountain path until he reached Seti.

What did you find?

Nothing down there, but the horse said we should follow him to his farm where he can share some food with us.

Seti looked to the sky.

I hope it isn't far. This snow is about to bury us!

Ghost and Seti remained a good distance away from the farmer's wagon as they followed it out of the city and into the surrounding countryside. The tracks from the wagon were deep, as the snow continued to fall. By now the trees had all lost their leaves, and their branches overhead created a lacey arbor, with the slate-grey sky above. Now and again, the wind would howl, sending a shiver through both of them. But the promise of food gave them reason to continue. They reached the outskirts of the farm by nightfall.

The two friends remained hidden behind an ancient tall tree with a wide trunk, watching as the farmer unhitched the horse from his wagon and led him into the barn. The great wooden structure was weathered, obviously having stood for many years. The planks on the siding were warped here and there, and the roof had a gaping hole where it had collapsed.

Still, it was shelter, and the snow was still falling. If Ghost and Seti could find relief from the elements, even for a single night, it would give them a chance to regain their energy for the continuing journey ahead.

The farmer appeared from inside the barn, pulled a large door closed, then trudged through the snow into his house. After a moment, a light appeared from inside the house, and before too long, smoke began curling from the chimney.

It looks safe now, Seti.

Why don't you go first, and make sure there aren't any small animals that I might frighten?

Okay – give me a minute…

Following the tracks of the wagon along the country road, Ghost approached the barn. When he arrived at the front door, he nudged it open with his nose, and then poked his head inside.

There was a large, open floor space with hay strewn about. Long wooden posts marked the dividing line between a row of stalls and a loft containing bales of hay stacked to the rafters. It was dark, but Ghost could see that the horse that had been pulling the milk wagon was in a stall, eating oats from a bucket.

In another stall was a long-eared donkey – smaller in stature from the horse by at least a foot. It was also eating. It looked up and saw Ghost staring at it, but gave no reaction, as if Ghost was the least interesting thing in the entire world. The donkey went right back to its evening meal.

Three cows were lined up in the same pen, behind a metal fence. Two of them were on the floor, asleep. The third chewed its cud, oblivious to its surroundings.

There was a chicken coop, with a half-dozen birds clucking softly, bobbing their heads and looking around the barn and at each other. They were sitting atop individual bunches of hay, obviously protecting the recently-laid eggs that lay beneath them.

In the last stall, against the back wall, was a tall, older horse with a grey coat and a grey mane. He too ate from his bucket, but he also kept a constant watch – with suspicious eyes – on the other animals in the barn. It seemed to Ghost that the old horse was on high alert, waiting for some other animal to try and take his food away from him.

Ghost eased the door open a bit further and stepped into the barn. The chickens immediately began clucking loudly in reaction to this strange animal. The donkey continued eating, disinterested, and the milk wagon horse lifted his head to greet Ghost.

I'm glad you didn't bring your...friend...with you – that would have created an even louder clatter than this!

Yes, he's waiting to see if it's safe for him to come inside.

The milk wagon horse jerked his head, indicating that Ghost should come closer. He spoke in hushed tones.

Tell him to climb the ramp on the outside of the barn, facing the road. That will lead to the loft, and he can sleep in the hay up there.

How will he find food?

That's no concern of mine. When the master comes for us in the morning, he'll guess that you simply wandered in from the snowstorm, and put you to work. He's a good human. He will treat you well.

Who invited you to our home?!

A voice boomed out from the corner of the barn. It was the old horse, Odessa and he took a few menacing steps forward, stomping his foot on the dirt floor.

You will not replace me on this farm! I am the lead horse! I am fed first! I am brushed and combed first!

The milk wagon horse tried to calm down the angry old horse.

Odessa! He is a traveler in need of shelter! He's not trying to take anything away from you or any of us!

It's a trick, and you are too stupid to see it, being a common milk horse. These clever wandering horses, they proclaim their innocent need, but then you watch helplessly as they slowly maneuver their way into your stall eating your food! I won't have it! I won't!

Ghost was afraid that the horse's loud neighing would disturb the farmer.

Maybe I should go... What if your master hears the noise and comes out?

My master is very old and cannot hear a thing; neither loud thunder nor a pebble falling to the ground. The only worry we have is that Odessa will give himself a very sore throat by yelling all night.

Well... let me go tell my friend how to reach the second level of the barn, then I'll come back. Perhaps there might be some oats to spare?

No worries, my friend. I'll share my meal with you.

Thank you!

Ghost left the barn, with Odessa's loud yelling ringing in his ears. Outside, the snow was drifting now, and Ghost had to lift his legs completely out of the snow to take a step. He found Seti shivering near the road.

See the long wooden plank leading to that small entryway? Go up there and you'll find some nice hay to sleep in.

Ahh, that's good news, Ghost! What about food?

Well, I'm afraid there might not be a way for you to eat

tonight. There are cows and chickens…and a very angry old horse named Odessa. If any of them see you, there will surely be an uproar.

My stomach is very empty, Ghost! Maybe if I just took one of the chickens…?

Seti! What about your vow to never use violence?

You're right, of course you're right!

Just come inside and I'll find a way to get some food to you.

Ghost trudged through the snow to the barn's opening as Seti began a perilous trek up the narrow plank. It was covered with ice and snow, and Seti's feet slipped from beneath him as he fought to reach the top. Every time he got about halfway up, the ice would cause him to slide back down. Finally, he got a running start and leaped onto the plank. His weight caused the plank to bow; he was able to jump into the barn through the opening, but the plank fell noisily to the ground! Seti looked to the ground and saw the plank had snapped in two. Now he was too high up to jump back down – if he was going to exit the barn, it might have to be by the front door.

He moved quietly in the hay, careful to avoid alerting the animals below of his presence. He saw Ghost enter the barn and push the wooden door closed behind him.

Back again to steal my food!

Odessa stomped and exhaled furiously through his nostrils.

Ghost ignored the old horse and instead approached the milk horse.

I spoke to my friend. He'll stay up there and we won't have any trouble.

Good. Here, I saved some oats for you. And an apple.

Thank you!

Ghost moved into the stall and began eating. He knew he should go slowly to make the meager amount of oats last, but he couldn't help himself. Within seconds, he had eaten the remaining oats, leaving the apple.

Friend, if you're not going to eat that apple, then I will!

Ghost pushed the apple toward the rear of the stall with his hind leg.

Oh no, I'm going to eat it! I just wanted to wait a bit and truly enjoy it.

Don't wait too long, or else the mice will get at it.

After an hour or so, with the interior of the barn in near-complete darkness, the farm animals were all fast asleep. Ghost cautiously moved out of the stall and looked up, whispering.

Seti? Are you there?

Within a few seconds, Seti peered over a stack of hay.

I'm here!

I have an apple for you! But I have to figure out how to get it up there!

Maybe I could come down…?

No! It's too dangerous!!

Ghost looked all around the barn. In the darkness, it was hard to see, but he noticed a pitchfork leaning against the wall. It gave him an idea.

Ghost stepped carefully forward, making sure to avoid stepping on anything that might make a noise. When Odessa stomped his foot on the ground, Ghost froze in his tracks, afraid the old horse had spotted him! But Odessa was still asleep, and was moving slightly as he slept.

Ghost let out a sigh of relief and continued toward the pitchfork. He opened his mouth and bit down hard on the wooden handle, and dragged it back to his stall. Seti watched with great interest as his friend seemed to be raking the stray bits of hay on the dirt floor.

But then Ghost's plan became clear. He kicked the apple into the center of the barn and then stabbed it with one of the sharp tines of the pitchfork. He then maneuvered the wooden handle so the sharp metal tines were over his head. Moving like an acrobat, Ghost held the pitchfork closer and closer to Seti until the wolf could take the apple in his mouth!

Got it!

Seti disappeared behind the haystack. Ghost could hear the crunch of the apple, as Seti began devouring it. Ghost loudly whispered to his friend.

Chew quietly!

Seti adjusted his eating style, and ate the rest of the apple without making any more noise. When he was finished, he looked down at Ghost.

Thank you!

You're welcome!

Just then, one of the chickens started stirring in its coop. Seti ducked, and Ghost moved back into his stall. The chicken remained asleep, and soon both Ghost and Seti fell into a welcome slumber.

It was still dark outside when the barn door was pulled open, revealing the old farmer, wearing a heavy coat and knee-high boots. He looked around for the pitchfork, but couldn't find it.

"Now where did I put that pitchfork…? Ahh, here it is!" The old farmer spotted the pitchfork on the ground, near Ghost's stall. He leaned down to pick it up and noticed Ghost.

"What have we here? How did you get in the barn, stranger?" The old farmer examined Ghost, opening his mouth and checking out his flank. "You're not one of mine, and you don't belong to my neighbors…"

Odessa awoke with a start and noticed the old farmer standing near Ghost.

Beware! He's coming to ruin your farm, human! He'll kick in your doors and trample your garden! I've seen it before! Many, many times!

The farmer noticed that Odessa was upset.

"What's gotten into you, old one?" The farmer moved close to Odessa and began rubbing his neck. "Stop your fussing, it's just a horse. We can use the extra help come spring, don't you think?" The old farmer moved to a stack of hay bales in the barn and began lifting them into the

horses' stalls.

"Here you go, here's breakfast!" In each stall, the farmer loosened the bales and scattered the hay in front of the horses.

Don't feed the new horse! He means to do you harm!

Odessa kept a panicked eye on the old farmer as he moved from stall to stall, feeding the horses. The farmer gave hay to the milk horse and then to Ghost.

No! It's a mistake!

The milk horse shook his head at Odessa.

You're going to make yourself sick, yelling like that first thing in the morning!

You're in on it too! I'm sure of it! You're both plotting against me and everyone on this farm!

The milk horse turned to Ghost as the farmer continued feeding the other animals.

Odessa will grow tired of himself soon. Just eat your hay and try not to listen.

Ghost began eating the hay while keeping thoughts of Seti close in his mind. He knew it must be hard for his friend to hear everyone talking about food, when he didn't have any himself.

In the loft, Seti was paying attention to something completely different – in one of the fields he'd spotted several rabbits hopping toward the country road. Overhead, a grey barn owl flapped its enormous wings, circling the rabbits below.

Seti watched intently as the owl swooped toward the rabbits, its talons outstretched, ready to snatch its helpless prey. The owl dove toward the largest rabbit – a floppy-eared, brown male – and just barely missed latching onto it! The rabbit managed to outrun the owl by a pace or two, and raced away in a zig-zag pattern, making it more difficult for the owl to follow its path.

Seti's stomach growled. Despite his vow of non-violence, he was still hungry, and rabbits were a common and welcome meal for any wolf. But for the moment, Seti was stuck high above the field, and he was curious to see how the encounter would play out below.

The owl changed direction and began following two smaller rabbits – a white one and one with tan spots. Both were young, Seti could tell, and while they had a lot of energy, their legs weren't very long yet, making it difficult for them to run fast.

The owl swooped and managed to grab the white rabbit in its talons, flapping furiously to rise in the air so it could take its meal away and eat in solitude. But the rabbit kicked and twisted itself so frantically that the owl lost its grip. The young rabbit tumbled through the air and landed in a snow bank, completely disappearing below the surface.

After a moment, the snow started shifting and the white rabbit suddenly popped through and immediately began running toward the country road. Meanwhile, the owl had shifted back to the larger rabbit, which had run itself directly into the middle of a frozen pond. The surface was slippery and, try as it might, the rabbit couldn't gain any traction. It slipped and slid, becoming more and more frantic as the owl circled overhead.

Then, out of the corner of Seti's eye, came a streak of rust-red, heading for the frozen pond. It was a mature fox, and its body was vivid against the blinding white snowy ground. The owl, having seen the fox running, adjusted its flight and instead dove for the fox. They collided on the snow, with the owl trying to tear at the fox's neck with its sharp beak and talons, and the fox biting the owl on its body and legs. Tufts of fur flew in the air as the two creatures attacked each other, and soon the white snow was being sprinkled with the bright red blood seeping from their wounds.

The rabbit was still doing its best to scamper off the ice and to safety, but its fear caused it to try too hard; it fell again and again. The other rabbits had raced to the country road and disappeared in a thicket of bushes. Seti wondered how long the rabbit could survive on the ice.

The fight was coming to a close. The owl had done its damage to the fox, but the fox had managed to inflict even greater wounds; one of the owl's wings hung limp at its side, having been torn at its root. As the owl struggled to escape, the fox clamped onto its leg with sharp teeth and held fast.

The owl fought to escape, but it was quickly losing energy. Eventually, it collapsed to the ground and within seconds, the fox was on it. The fox made quick work of its meal, leaving behind only feathers and a bloody smear on the snow.

Seti watched as the fox slunk away into the forest. His hunger had grown greater than ever. He glanced at the frozen pond and saw the rabbit sitting there, helpless. Seti's instincts took over his reason, and without any hesitation, he leaped from the barn loft to the soft snow below.

In a daze, Seti moved close to the snowy ground toward the pond. The rabbit looked up and saw yet another predator coming toward it and it fought helplessly to escape its fate. Seti had no problem walking on the ice; as a young pup, he had mastered the art of maintaining his balance on slippery surfaces. He had become a master at stalking his prey, whether they were on dry land, wet rocks or ice.

As he approached the rabbit, he hesitated. There was stark fear in the rabbit's eyes. Seti was beyond hungry – and a rabbit meal would be a most welcome thing. But something inside of Seti spoke louder than his hunger. He remembered the vow he had made to give up violence no matter what.

All of Seti's wolf instincts told him to bite the rabbit's

neck, give it a good shake, killing it, and then eat his meal. But another part of Seti – a kind of wisdom and understanding that he felt in the deepest part of his heart – gave him another message.

He moved closer to the rabbit and opened his mouth. He took the rabbit's neck between his teeth, but instead of biting down, he gently carried it across the frozen ice to the pond's bank. With a slight nod, Seti allowed the rabbit to fall out of his mouth to the frozen ground below. The rabbit looked up at him, dazed and still shaking. When it became clear that Seti was not going to kill it, the rabbit rose to its feet, raced across the country road and into the bushes. Seti watched it go without a single regret.

Seven

"Come on, Odessa, let's get you some exercise!" The old farmer eased the horse from its stall and out of the barn. "I know it's cold, but you need to move those legs or else they'll go stiff; that's for sure!"

Odessa wasn't the least bit interested in anything the farmer had to say. He was more intent on keeping his eye on Ghost.

Do not enter my stall, do you hear me? That is my home, not yours!

He continued his tirade as the farmer led him into a pen next to the barn. There, Odessa could walk or run – there was room for both. Once the old horse felt the fresh air on his face, he surrendered to his instincts and began running in the snow. It felt good to move. In his younger days, Odessa performed most of the duties of helping to run the farm. He pulled wagons, lugged timber and allowed the farmer to ride him throughout the valley. Now that he and the farmer were older, there were fewer needs to work the land. The farmer kept a small vegetable garden near his house, from which he canned food to last him the winter. He also kept meat in a cold-storage locker behind his house, food that came from the previous autumn's hunting season.

Inside the barn, the milk horse turned to Ghost.

I don't hear your friend up in the loft. Are you sure he's there?

He was yesterday, but I haven't heard anything either. Seti! Are you there?

All was quiet in the barn except for the soft clucking from the chickens. The donkey lifted his head briefly to see what was going on but, finding nothing worthwhile, returned to staring at the ground.

Maybe he left to find food?

Ghost nodded. He was sure what Seti had done.

Maybe I should go look for him.

Why not wait until the farmer takes me into town? He'll have his milk ready for delivery soon and Odessa will be in the field. All you have to do is make sure that none of the other animals see your friend.

I don't know how I can repay your kindness.

No need. I was a stray when I first came to this farm. The old man took me in and gave me work and shelter. Passing along the kindness is the least I can do.

And so Ghost waited patiently until the old farmer came to hitch the milk horse to his wagon. He approached Ghost.

"Well, you look strong, don't you? How'd you like to stay here on the farm and work for me? I'll need some help repairing those fence posts along the road; you can carry that load for me, can't you?" The farmer gave him a pat and went to hitch the milk horse to the wagon.

Ghost waited until he could no longer hear the wagon on the country road, as it made its way into the village. He carefully stepped toward the barn door, keeping an eye out for Odessa, who was still in the field. The old horse was far away, toward a slope where the farm acreage met a stand of trees.

Ghost quickly exited the barn and galloped to the far side, out of Odessa's line of vision. He scanned the horizon for some sign of Seti, but all he could see was an unusual red stain halfway between the barn and the road, scattered across the snow. Filled with fear that Seti may have been injured, Ghost stepped carefully toward what he discovered was blood. The sight sent a wave of shock through him, but he felt relief when he saw bird's feathers. He thought perhaps Seti had gotten into a fight with another animal, but he saw no wolf tracks anywhere near the blood.

However, he soon heard a loud neighing coming from the other side of the barn. He galloped to where Odessa was racing back and forth behind a wooden fence, while staring intently at the farmer's house.

It's a wolf! I knew you would bring bad luck to this farm! First you come and steal my food; now a wolf has invaded, ready to kill us all!

Calm down, Odessa! Maybe it was just a dog…

It was a wolf! What do you take me for, a fool? Next thing you know, the old farmer will abandon us all and we'll be left to starve in the snow! This is your doing! I knew it the minute I saw you! Nothing but trouble!

I'll go see what's happening – maybe the wolf has gone already!

Have you lost your senses? That wolf will take you down and eat you, sure as I'm standing here!

Well, maybe that would solve at least one of your problems, right Odessa?

You're not the least bit frightened?

Of course I am – but I'll do it for you. Just to prove that I mean you no harm.

Odessa was stunned into silence. Ghost had to suppress a laugh as he walked toward the house.

Ghost could hear scratching noises coming from the rear of the farmer's small house. There, he found his friend attempting to gain access to the outside meat locker, where the old farmer kept his winter food.

Seti! What are you doing?

There's food in here, Ghost! And I'm starving!

I'm not sure stealing is a good idea. That old farmer, he seems like a good human.

I won't take all of it, just enough to help me survive.

What happened in the field? I saw blood...

It was an owl chasing rabbits. Then a fox came and attacked.

Sounds like you've had a busy day.

Ghost – I...had one of the rabbits in my control, but I didn't eat it. I let it go.

Ghost could barely believe his ears. Seti, under the painful grip of hunger, gave up a captive meal.

It would have been so easy just to… Well, I guess I'm seeing the world in a new way.

Ghost nodded. He took a step forward, near the locker.

Here, let me help you.

Ghost used his body weight to press against the wood. Within seconds, it cracked slightly – just enough to allow Seti to pull down a slab of meat hanging on hooks.

Ghost, go back to the barn – I'll cover your tracks with my own so the farmer doesn't know you were here helping me!

I don't think you should bring that meat back to the barn.

I couldn't even if I wanted to – there's no way for me to get back up to the loft.

But where will you go?

I'll find a place. Wolves are pretty smart, you know!

Ghost peered around the corner, making sure Odessa couldn't see him, and then he hurried to return to the barn. Seti walked back and forth, on top of Ghost's hoof prints and then, with the meat in his jaws, he followed Ghost's tracks to the barn, covering them with his own.

It was early evening when the old farmer returned with his milk wagon. He unhitched the horse and led him into the stall, then went to the field to bring Odessa back in from his day-long excursion. Odessa kept up his nonstop monologue.

There was a wolf! A wolf!! Of course it came at the same

*time you let this evil horse come into the barn! Don't you realize
what you've done? This is the beginning of the end of us all!*

The farmer noticed that Odessa was pulling and tugging
on his lead.

"Easy old fella, what's gotten into you? Have I left you
too long in the snow?" The farmer eased Odessa into his
stall and reached for his pitchfork. "It's food you want, isn't
it? I know a hungry horse when I see one!"

Odessa continued his outburst.

*Foolish human! Along with the rest of the lazy animals
on this farm! Is it so hard to understand when you are
being attacked?*

The milk horse stomped its legs on the ground.

*That's enough, Odessa! You're upsetting everyone and for no
good reason!*

There was a wolf here today!

*I don't see it now, so that must mean it's gone! Now behave
yourself, or I'll come over there and give you a bite you won't
soon forget!*

The old farmer, unaware of the conversation between the
horses, continued preparing their hay. Odessa, stung by the
milk horse's words, stared at him with increasing intensity.

Give me a bite, will you? We'll see about that!

Odessa leaped out of his stall and brushed past the
farmer, spinning him around to the ground. He head-butted
the milk horse, sending him backward in his stall. Ghost
attempted to stand in between them.

Stop it! What are you fighting for?

You're all in it against me, that's what you are! But you forget, I'm Odessa, I've been here the longest, and you won't easily take my place!

Odessa moved forward to attack the milk horse again. But the milk horse had regained its senses and reared onto its hind legs, kicking at Odessa.

Go back to your stall, Odessa, you're going to get hurt! You'll be more than hurt!

Odessa spun around just as the old farmer was regaining his feet. One of Odessa's hind legs kicked the farmer in the head. There was a sickening crack, and the farmer's eyes rolled back in his head. He collapsed to the ground, unmoving.

All was silent in the barn for a moment. Then Odessa backed into his stall.

It's your fault! Don't you dare blame me!

The milk horse took a step forward.

He's bleeding. What should we do?

The donkey, who had remained silent the past few days, lifted its head.

There's another farm just down the road. Take him there. But how?

Ghost paced back and forth, thinking. He felt partly responsible for this calamity, even though it was Odessa who started the fight. An idea came to him, but it was one filled with hazards. He turned to the milk horse.

I need to find my friend. He can help lift the farmer onto my back!

Then do it! Hurry!

I have to tell you something first. My friend…he's a wolf.

The milk horse's eyes widened in fear. Odessa leaped forward.

I knew it! You're the devil! You brought a wolf into our midst! And now look where we are!

Ghost wheeled around and faced Odessa directly.

Listen to me well, because I'm only going to say this once. This is your fault. You did this. We all know it and no amount of lies from your lips will change that. Do you understand?

Odessa was silent.

I'm going to bring my friend here. He won't harm any of you so don't make everyone upset with your lies!

But a wolf…!

If you only believe what you already know, you're not going to learn very much in this lifetime. We'll take the farmer down the road and see that he receives the help he needs. And when we return, you'd better think twice before you cause any more trouble!

Ghost moved directly in front of Odessa until the old horse could feel his breath.

I realize you are old and frightened. That does not excuse you from your behavior. You can help. Or you can cause trouble. Choose wisely.

Ghost turned and exited the barn. The milk horse stared

at Odessa, daring him to say something. The old horse could do nothing but hang his head in shame.

It took several attempts to lift the old farmer onto Ghost's back, but eventually Ghost was able to straighten up as the farmer's body hung limply on top. Odessa had remained deep in his stall, silently watching as Seti helped drag the human. The other animals in the barn were quiet and subdued, aware of the seriousness of the farmer's wound. If he were to die, the very fate of the animals was in jeopardy.

The milk horse gave Ghost and Seti some final instructions.

I don't know much about the neighbor down the road, only that he sells his vegetables in town during the summer. Bring the old farmer to him, maybe he'll be able to help. It's our only chance.

Ghost nodded and moved slowly out of the barn. The snow had begun falling again and the wind was whipping the already-fallen snow into huge drifts. Seti walked alongside, keeping an eye out for predators.

This way, Ghost! We can take a shortcut across the field! There's a path next to the frozen pond!

How do you know?

I came this way earlier; it's where the rabbits were running away from the owl.

Ghost plodded through the deep snow, his head down against the onslaught of the strong winds. Each step was difficult, as his legs sunk more than a foot. Every now and then, the wind would blow so strongly that he and Seti were pushed nearly off their feet. Still, they pressed on, determined to reach the other farm and save the old human.

Overhead, there was a loud cracking sound. They looked up just in time to see a large branch, overloaded with snow and ice, falling toward them! Ghost was able to dodge the branch just in time as it crashed next to him. Had it hit him, he would surely have been seriously hurt, and possibly killed.

We need to stay away from these trees, Seti! I'm going back onto the road!

You're right – maybe the snow won't be as deep as it is in the field!

They struggled to climb a short hill that led to the road. A barbed-wire fence stood between them and their objective; Seti was able to make it easily through two strands, but Ghost's task was more difficult. He carefully lifted one leg at a time over the sharp barbs, but some of them still managed to cut into his flesh.

Ghost, are you okay?

I'm fine, just as long as I don't drop him onto the snow…

Finally Ghost was able to lift his rear leg over the fence and make his way to the road. The snow was much less deep there and so they were able to make better progress on their way to the next farm.

Daylight was fading as the afternoon turned into evening, with no letup of the snowstorm. Finally, in the distance, they could see a light coming from a window in the farm house.

Seti, I see it! Up there!

With relief, Ghost picked up his pace, reaching a wooden gate near the road at the front of the property. It was a small wooden house, with white smoke curling from the chimney. Now that they were closer, they could see candlelight coming from several rooms, and a shadow of someone moving around inside.

What should we do?

Take the farmer to the front of the house – we'll ease him to the ground and then we can make noise so they'll come out and find him.

Ghost carried the old farmer onto the porch. The wooden slats creaked as he bent forward, allowing the man to slip gently down. But before Ghost and Seti could back away, the front door opened, revealing a human holding a rifle!

"Who's there?" He bellowed loudly, but was struck dumb at the sight of a horse and a wolf on his front porch. He looked down and saw the farmer – his neighbor – lying at his feet, a bloody wound on his head.

He called to someone in the house. "A wolf attacked old George next door! He's lying on the porch, half-dead! Grab a rifle!"

The man brought his weapon up to his shoulder and aimed at Seti. The wolf barely had time to register what was happening, but in a split-second, he ducked to the right as the human fired! The bullet missed Seti by less than an inch.

Seti and Ghost raced from the house, toward the road.

"They're getting away!" The human took aim and fired again, this time hitting the gate, sending pieces of wood splintering. Ghost and Seti continued running as fast as they could. The human kept shooting at them until they disappeared beyond the horizon.

Eight

The two friends had run for nearly an hour, just in case the human had decided to follow them. They were exhausted. Their lungs were in pain from breathing in the frigid air and their limbs felt like they were on fire.

Seti noticed a structure on a ridge in the distance.

Come on, Ghost – maybe we can rest in there!

As they came closer, they could see the structure was a railroad car attached to a longer series of rusted metal cars.

No, Seti. Those things are dangerous!

But it's just sitting here, and it will protect us from the cold!

All right…but just for a little while…until the snow stops falling.

Seti leaped into the car and looked all around. It was empty except for an old blanket that someone had left.

It looks safe, Ghost!

Ghost nodded and climbed into the railroad car. It was dusty and dirty, and it smelled like smoke. But Ghost was glad to be standing on something that wasn't frozen snow, giving his legs a chance to warm.

Why did that human try to kill us back there?

Why do humans do anything that they do? None of it makes sense.

Maybe he thought we were the ones who hurt his friend.

That's silly. Why would we bring him for help if we were the ones who hurt him?

I don't know. Trying to understand humans makes my head hurt.

They settled themselves as best they could, with Seti curling up in the blanket. It smelled like rotting fish, but Seti ignored that and was grateful for the small degree of warmth it provided.

The night was silent. Outside, the snow finally stopped, and the wind subsided. The now-clear sky was filled with stars and Seti gazed at them, his heart full of longing for his mate.

I wonder what Luna is doing. We've been gone a long time.

I know. I'm sorry for asking you to come along on this terrible journey.

You've already apologized, Ghost. And I've told you to stop doing that. I'm here because I wanted to come with you.

What if the castle doesn't exist? I don't want to believe it, but I suppose it's possible that my father was just telling tall tales.

If the castle isn't there, then we've at least had an incredible adventure together.

But how long should we continue before we decide it's been long enough?

We'll know. Somehow we'll know.

Seti's eyes were filled with the deep orange and crimson of the rising sun. He inhaled deeply, having slept soundly for nearly ten hours. His body had been so hungry for rest, and now that it was morning, it was also hungry for food. Maybe they could find another farm soon – but this time they would try not to be seen by humans or animals. It was simply too dangerous.

Before he could rise to his feet, Seti felt the train car jerk forward. His eyes widened as he felt movement beneath his body! He looked outside and saw that the train was starting to move!

Ghost! Wake up! Wake up!

Ghost opened his eyes and blinked several times.

What is it?

The train is moving! We have to jump off!

Ghost, who had been lying down with his rear legs tucked beneath him, struggled to rise. The train started moving faster, and was now picking up speed.

Ghost! Now!

I'm trying! It's not easy to lift this big body up!

By the time Ghost had risen to his feet, the train was speeding forward too quickly for them to jump. They could see the countryside whiz past them. Seti couldn't believe his eyes.

I've never gone this fast before!

It's too fast, Seti! Somebody could get hurt!

What are we going to do, Ghost? Who knows where this thing will take us?

I guess we'll just have to wait and find out…

The train mostly kept at a steady pace while it was on a long straightaway. Occasionally, it wound around curves that made the train cars veer to the left or to the right. Ghost felt dizzy when this happened – it seemed as though his stomach would drop right out of his body.

As the day wore on, Ghost and Seti continued their vigil. The countryside changed from grassy to rocky as the train seemed to be going higher and higher. Soon, they could see vast distances, and it became apparent that the train was climbing up a mountain.

Hillsides gave way to great, tall cliffs and rocky outposts. There was barely any vegetation at this altitude, only stones and boulders half-covered in snow and ice. The metal gears of the train scraped and wheezed as the tracks wound in snake patterns through the mountain.

At one point, the train passed through a dark tunnel. Ghost and Seti were momentarily frightened, believing the sun itself had suddenly gone dark! But soon they were through the tunnel and back on their climb up the mountain.

As the track evened out in a straight line, the train slowed, and they heard a loud whistle come from some place near the front of the train cars. The train was passing by a village nestled in the mountain. There were a dozen or so small houses with thatched roofs and white-coated sheep idling in bunches.

In the distance, Seti could see a large stone structure

with spires seeming to reach into the clouds.

Ghost, is that the castle?

No. It doesn't look like the one my father described.

Humans really like to build castles, don't they?

They fight to gain territory, then they have to build castles and walls to defend the territory they fought for while somebody else tries to take it away from them.

I've seen young wolf pups do that. One of them steals a bone and then the others try to take it away from them. But most of the time, when they get a little older and wiser, they stop playing that game.

Humans don't ever seem to stop. The bone they fight over just gets bigger.

The train continued rattling through the mountains, revealing breathtaking views of snow-capped mountain ranges and the valleys below. Ghost and Seti marveled at the sight of goats clinging to the sides of sheer rock walls, jumping onto small footholds, never missing a beat.

One morning, the train whistle blew loudly and the train itself started to slow down to a crawl. It finally stopped; Ghost and Seti were on high alert, keeping a watchful eye out for humans.

Maybe this is where the trains stops, then it has to go back down the mountain?

Well, we've been traveling toward the sunrise most of the way, so at least we've been heading in the right direction.

Just then, they heard the sound of footsteps crunching

on the snow outside. A human walked past the open train car, and a moment later, returned. He was young, with a heavy coat and stocking cap, leather gloves and work boots. He stared at the train car in disbelief.

"What in the world…? Shoo! Go on now, get out of here, this is no place for animals! Scatter, you hear me!?"

The man waved his hat at Ghost and Seti, who dodged and ducked, then finally leapt over the man completely onto the snowy ground below. They ran away before the man could grab them and followed the path of the tracks ahead.

On one side of them was a rocky cliff and beyond it, a range of mountains that seemed to reach to the sky itself. On the other side was a hill leading to valleys already dark because the sunlight was blocked out by the surrounding mountains. Here and there, they spotted houses and farms, but this time they weren't tempted to investigate, having

found occasional edible herbs and berries next to the
train tracks.

As night began to fall, they were suddenly aware of a
bird swooping near their heads, then flying away and
returning again. It came from various directions, as if it
didn't have a clue where it was going.

The bird finally landed directly on Ghost's back.

*Ta-daa! That's what you're supposed to say when you do
something amazing! What did you think about my landing?
Perfect, wasn't it? Ta-daa!*

The bird's voice sounded more like a loud child than
a grownup animal.

Should we introduce ourselves?

Ghost and Seti stared at the strange bird.

*Okay, I'll go first. I'm a bird. You probably figured that out
already! To be more precise, I'm a loon! Did you ever meet a
loon before? We're friendly! Well, to be more precise, most of us
are friendly. Some loons I've met, hoo boy, you don't want to get
in their way if they're in a bad mood! Not to say they're bad
birds, mind you. Anyone can have a bad day! Take me for*

instance...well to be more precise, don't actually take me. Just listen to me, that's what I meant. Are you following me?

Ghost looked at Seti, then back at the loon.

What exactly are you trying to say?

I'm welcoming you to Germany!

What is a Germany?

It's a country! You've heard of countries? Germany is one of them! Actually, somewhere around here is Leichtenstein, that's another country; it's back that way. You probably walked right through it. Did you like it? I've never been, but I hear it's beautiful this time of year! Did I mention that I'm a loon?

Seti couldn't take his eyes off the strange creature.

Yes, you did. You're a loon. I'm a wolf and this is a horse.

I knew it! I said to myself, if that's not a wolf and a horse, then I'll jump right into a freezing cold lake. And let me tell you, I'm pretty glad I was right because to be honest, I'm not a big fan of cold water. So! What should we do now?

Ghost took a few steps forward.

First of all, you can get off my back. We...are going to keep walking. What you do is your business.

The loon leapt to the ground and sidled up to Seti.

Where are you going? Can I go with you?

Why would you want to come with us if you don't know where we're going?

Hmm...let me think about that. If I don't know where you're going...then I...oh, I know! It's because I like to go to new places! Tell me you're going someplace new! Oh please oh please oh please!

Seti exhaled deeply, becoming annoyed at this babbling bird.

If you must know, we're on our way to find an amazing castle. It's many years old and it's the most beautiful castle in the whole world.

I know that castle! I do!

The loon did a silly dance, prancing in a circle in the snow, then tossing its body into the air, landing on its rear end.

I can show you! I can take you there!

Is that so?

Ghost was skeptical. He wasn't about to put his trust in a silly creature like this, not after all the hardship they'd faced.

Oh yes! I fly there all the time. You know, there are a lot of birds that roost in the towers. And those towers, my goodness, there are lots of them! With colorful flags flying from them, and oh, the size of the castle will take your breath away. To be more specific, it won't actually do that; you won't run out of breath, but I'm pretty sure you'll like what you see! Can I come? Say yes!

Ghost and Seti exchanged glances.

Ghost, it does sound like he knows what he's talking about…

Ghost cocked his head and gave Seti a doubtful look.

Well, you know what I mean. He's…kind of unusual…but maybe he could lead us to the castle. Isn't it worth a try?

As long as we keep moving toward the sunrise, I suppose it couldn't hurt. All right, bird, you can come. But don't talk so much, all right?

I won't! I'll be as silent as a rock! You won't hear a sound coming from me! Even if I fall down and hurt myself, I won't cry out in pain! I'll do this – watch!

The bird sat staring at Ghost with its mouth shut.

Like that, okay? The Quiet Loon, that's what you'll call me!

The unusual trio proceeded along the train track until the loon said they should veer off-course and follow a path that led into a valley. Ghost wasn't sure.

Wait – why are we going down? I was told that the castle was on a mountain.

The loon stared at Ghost with its mouth shut. Ghost rolled his eyes.

You may speak.

Thank you! I thought I would burst, I have so much to say! Yes, you are correct, the castle is high on a mountain, but if we cross into the valley this way, we'll save a lot of time going up and down and up and down, oh these trails can be exhausting, let me tell you!

So we go into the valley, then back up over there, to that mountain?

Down then up! What could be easier? Oh, and don't worry about food in the valley! See, the snow doesn't reach all the way down, because these trees, see them? They keep the snow off the ground and that means bushes and berries and herbs keep growing pretty much all year round! I'll bet you didn't know that, did you?

Without responding, Ghost and Seti made their way down the path, toward the valley. The bird realized that they had already made up their minds and scrambled to follow them.

Okay, you're going into the valley! Got it! Here I come!

It was difficult to see very far in front of them, as the valley was shrouded in near complete darkness. Seti, with his excellent night vision, led the way, calling out to Ghost when there were loose rocks or twists and turns on the pathway.

The loon kept up a running commentary as they made their way down.

I saw a bear here one time, ooh it was mean, with teeth as big as a tree! But was I scared? Ha! I don't know the meaning of the word scared! I mean, I do know the meaning, of course it means frightened, but what I meant was that fear means nothing to me! Bears don't scare me – you should have seen how I chased him away! I said, bear, you are bothering the wrong bird because even though you're bigger than me and stronger than me and your teeth are sharper, I have something you don't have!

The bird stopped talking. Ghost turned around to face the loon.

Finish your story.
I did!
You said you told the bear you had something he didn't have! Like what?

I don't know, it was your story!

Hmm…let me see…maybe it was wings?

Is that what you told him?

Could be…

Seti and Ghost looked tired and annoyed.

Maybe you should just stop talking…

Okay, but wait – we're supposed to go this way!

Ghost stopped walking and looked up.

No, we just came that way…

No offense, horse, but I live here in this valley, I should know where the castle is!

Seti sniffed the ground in front of them.

Then maybe you can explain why our scent is already on that path.

Yes, and our tracks!

Ghost and Seti stared at the loon, expecting an answer. The bird looked down, as if it was caught in a lie.

Maybe you're right…but it's getting dark now and it could be dangerous climbing the mountain before morning.

What do you propose?

We could sleep outside…in the freezing cold…but I happen to know there's a nice warm snug cave, just over there, where we can be safe! Come on, I'll show you!

The loon hurried into a thicket of trees and disappeared in the darkness. Ghost and Seti watched him go.

Ghost, what do you want to do?

I don't think we have any choice. Let's spend the night in

the cave and then we'll see about tomorrow morning.

The cave was small, but the loon was right – it was warm and kept them safe from the snow and wind. It was a tight fit – Ghost had to keep his head part of the way out of the cave.

The loon paced back and forth in the tiny space available to it on the floor.

What's your problem, bird?

Huh? Oh, no problem, no problem at all! I'm just…I'm hungry! When I'm hungry I can't sit still!

But you ate berries when we did. In fact, I think you ate more than Ghost and me combined!

That's what I meant to say – I ate too much. You know what, I'm feeling a little restless! Can't go to sleep if my stomach is too full, right? Okay, so I'll be back in a little while, you both stay here and you'll be warm and safe and then I'll be back in a little while!

You just said that.

I did? Oh yes, right you are! Well, enjoy the cave and goodbye!

With that, the loon raced out of the cave and scampered into the forest. Ghost watched him, a look of curiosity on his face.

What was that all about?

Well, he is a loon, after all…

With the bird gone, Ghost could now settle more comfortably in the small cave space. He adjusted himself to the ground and got comfortable.

One more night, lost in the world somewhere, eh Seti?

It could be worse, Ghost. We could be lost in our own homes.

What do you mean?

When Ramses died, I didn't know what to do. My life had been turned upside down. The day before it happened, I knew who I was, and what my life was about. The day after, it all disappeared. Nothing mattered. Nothing made sense.

That must have been so hard for you, Seti.

It's the worst thing. But on this journey – this impossible, nonsensical journey – with my best friend, somehow I'm finding myself again. It's more than just changing scenery or location. It's more than having adventures and testing my strength. It's about making a connection with the world. Stepping into unknown lands and becoming part of them. Running and eating and feeling cold and tired – and then starting over the next day with strength and excitement. I don't know, it makes me feel alive.

Seti gazed directly into Ghost's eyes.

My friend, I don't know if we will ever find that castle of yours and I don't care. This quest has given me a reason to wake up in the morning. It's given me my life back.

Ghost nodded silently. Seti's words reached a deep part of his heart and he was filled with gratitude for this unlikely friendship and all that came with it.

Nine

The next morning, Seti heard a crackling noise coming from outside the cave. His ears perked up, and he rose quickly, on high alert. But his sense of danger dimmed when he saw it was only the loon, poking his head from around the corner.

Oh, you're still here! Both of you! Well, that's really good news! I'm glad that —

The loon's words were cut short when something batted him out of the way, sending the bird sprawling into some bushes. The hair on Seti's neck bristled, and he bared his fangs.

Ghost woke up and rose to his feet.

Seti, what is it?

A deep, guttural voice emerged from the dark of the forest.

You've done your job, loon. Now go!

Dazed and in pain, the bird rose slowly. He looked at Seti and Ghost with shame.

I'm sorry…he made me!

I said go!

With that, the loon turned and fled into the forest,

leaving feathers floating to the ground in his wake.

From the darkness, a large creature moved forward. It was a wild boar, with two sharp, curved tusks jutting from his mouth. He was muscular and his skin was horribly scarred – remnants of many battles fought. On his clubbed feet were razor-sharp claws, which dug into the earth when he flexed. His breath was heavy and deep – with every exhalation, a cloud of malodorous condensation appeared.

But it was the boar's eyes that were most unsettling. They were blood-red and menacing, with an intensity that made it impossible for Ghost and Seti to look away. It was as if his very gaze held them in its power.

In the cave, the two friends were motionless, unsure of what to do next. Seti looked beyond the boar, hoping to find some way to escape. The boar noticed.

Look as you might, wolf. Even if you manage to race past me – which I doubt – this valley is as familiar to me as my own body. There is nowhere to run. Nowhere to hide. You are my meal for this day. And the horse shall feed me the whole of the coming week. It isn't often that fortune smiles upon me as such. It would be ungrateful of me to refuse it.

Ghost summoned the courage to speak directly to the boar.

We do not mean to tread on your land. We offer no disrespect. It was only our intention to sleep here one night and then be on our way.

Your words interest me not. It is your flesh that lures me.

Seti could sense that Ghost was trembling. He turned to look up at his friend.

I'm going to fight him.

Seti, no...your vow...

I won't let him hurt you. Not without a fight.

The boar let out a laugh that echoed throughout the valley.

The wolf challenges me! Now that is entertainment of the most excellent kind! You poor sad creature – there is no living thing in this valley or beyond that could match my strength. I've fought off three of my own kind at the same time – what threat could you pose that could rival that?

Seti looked directly into the boar's eyes.

This is what will happen. We will fight. And I will kill you. There is a place inside of you – hidden and secret – that knows my words are true. Despite your bluster and your foul words, you are frightened of me. I bid you to leave now and save yourself to trouble weaker creatures another day.

The boar took a step forward, shaking his head.

Me, afraid of you? Now I know – it was all a myth, this nonsense about the wisdom of wolves. Why, you're no more intelligent than the ridiculous bird who led me to you. Here, lay yourself down on the ground and offer me your neck. I'll make quick work of you. You won't feel anything beyond the first bite.

Seti inhaled and closed his eyes. In his mind he could see swirls and waves, as if he was floating on an ocean. Those were transformed into images of great, majestic wolves, all standing atop a mountain, radiating a kind of glowing aura that surrounded each one of them. The aura was many shades of red, like a changing sky at sunset and it grew into a floating cloud that resembled the Northern lights. It coalesced and floated toward Seti, enveloping him.

In the cave, Seti looked as if his entire body was being charged with electricity. His back arched, his head jerked, and his eyes rolled. A low moan started in his throat but grew in volume until it became a full-throated howl. It was so loud that the stone cave vibrated.

The boar was taken aback by this display, but only momentarily.

Your tricks are amusing, but enough! I'm hungry and you are going to die!

The boar charged at Seti, who remained in place, tucking his head down and bracing himself with his shoulder facing the boar. The boar, three times Seti's size, slammed into him with tremendous force, but Seti didn't move. In fact, it seemed as if he didn't feel the boar's weight at all!

The boar rolled to his side and stared at Seti, a look of disbelief on his face. He bared his fangs and attacked once again, this time taking Seti's neck in his mouth and biting down.

The boar maneuvered his body so he could put his full weight into pulling Seti out of the cave. Both animals spun around and fell to the ground. The boar quickly rose to his feet and stomped on Seti's flank with his heavy hooves. Seti let out a yelp of pain but quickly scrambled away and turned to face the boar again.

Seti feinted toward the boar, causing the beast to respond by moving to the left. But then Seti quickly lowered his head to the right and rammed the boar in its throat with all of his strength. The boar squealed and ducked, choking from the blow.

Ghost watched the battle with concern and fascination. He had seen Seti fight before, but never against such a tremendous opponent and certainly never with this intensity. He feared for his friend's life; it seemed impossible that Seti could ever overcome the boar's superior size.

The boar was able to duck its head and gore Seti's flank with one of its tusks. Seti felt a shock of pain race through his body like a blast of electricity. He looked up just in time to see the boar coming at him again. He leapt into the air and deflected most of the blow, but the boar was still able to send him spinning end over end. Dizzy, Seti landed in a heap and skidded down a small incline.

The boar wasted no time. Within seconds, he was attacking again, charging full-force at Seti. The wolf had enough presence of mind to spin on the ground, avoiding the fullness of the attack. But again, the boar was able to use its weight advantage effectively; as it passed Seti, it stomped on the wolf's hind leg, snapping the bone.

Ghost was startled by the sound of the breaking bone. A sick feeling washed over him as he saw his friend lying helpless on the ground.

Seti, run if you can! Run away!

The boar heard Ghost's cry and laughed.

He's not going anywhere except into my stomach! And then it'll be your turn!

But before the boar could turn to face Seti again, he was knocked off of his feet by a tremendous blow. Stunned, the boar looked up and saw Seti – limping, his breath ragged, blood covering his matted fur.

Your mistake…as with all predators…is in believing your own self-deception. Strength is more than force. Victory is greater than defeating an opponent. And in this very moment, your heart beats not with pride…but with fear because you finally understand that every bit of anger and hatred you have created is returning to you. I take no pleasure in becoming the instrument of your demise. But it must be, and so prepare yourself.

Seti, dragging his wounded leg, came closer to the boar,

who now gasped and blubbered, consumed with hysterical fear. In a final act of defiance, springing from somewhere deep in his rotten core, the boar bared his fangs and charged at Seti.

Ghost would never forget the images he saw next. Seti, much smaller than the boar, and severely wounded, met the charge head-on. The two animals gripped each other with all their strength, shoulder to shoulder, until Ghost could actually hear more bones breaking.

Seti moved deftly aside, allowing the boar's momentum to send it crashing into a nearby tree trunk. Seti swiftly turned and attacked, using his powerful jaws to grab hold of the boar's neck. Seti's eyes closed as he clenched down. The boar squirmed furiously, kicking at Seti's body with his hind legs. But Seti held on.

The boar fought and fought, blood spilling onto the ground. But slowly, as his life force ebbed out of his body, the boar slowed, and then stopped. It was over.

Seti, exhausted and in pain, rolled to the ground onto his back, breathing heavily. Ghost ran to his side.

Seti! What you did...it was...impossible! How...?

I don't know how, but I do know that every one of my ancestors was with me in the fight. So were you, and so were your parents.

Seti gazed into Ghost's eyes.

And so was my son. I felt him. Ramses' power and strength. Not the anger and hatred, but the passion he had when he was younger. Before he turned...

Come, let me help you to your feet. We can rest in the cave.

Wait – just let me say this. When we were fighting...I didn't hate the boar. Not at all. I felt...responsible for him...to kill him quickly and without humiliating him. I don't know... it's as if I respected him more by having to fight him. That's how I defeated him. Because he had to be defeated. He knew it too. That's why he attacked me. Does that make any sense?

I'm sure it will later. But for now, you'll rest.

The next morning, when Ghost opened his eyes, all he could see was a wall of grey. Standing, he realized that a thick fog had descended on the valley and into the cave. He glanced at Seti, who was still asleep. He thought he would let his friend get as much rest as possible after last night's fight with the boar.

Ghost wandered through the forest, allowing the strangeness of the heavy fog to wash over his body. It was like being underwater, but he also had the feeling of floating in the air. There were so few recognizable landmarks around him – he couldn't see the trees until they were within inches of his nose.

Overhead, he heard the sound of a bird cawing; it wasn't the loon, but rather a large bird of prey of some sort. Ghost had grown accustomed to hearing them back home, when they were circling for food, or alerting their families to potential danger.

This was no cry of danger though, the sound was too

easy and relaxed. Even though Ghost could not see the bird, he could tell it was spinning in lazy circles in the sky. Perhaps it was enjoying the sensation of flying through the fog.

Ghost heard Seti stirring; he hurried back to the cave and found his friend standing, although somewhat shakily.

How are you feeling today, Seti?

Considering what happened yesterday, I feel lucky to be alive!

Seti moved forward a few steps; his right hind leg curled under.

It's not a bad break, I'm sure of that. A few days taking it easy and I'll be good as new. That's an impressive fog – did you try to walk into the forest?

Yes, but I didn't get far. I'm wondering if it would be better for us to get out of this valley as soon as we can. Climb above the fog so we know where to go.

Well, I'll do my best but we'll have to go slowly. I'm not as young as I used to be, you know.

They found some meager berry bushes that yielded just enough food for the morning trek up the mountain. At first the ground was soft and easy to navigate; pine needles were scattered in big heaps, making for a comfortable pace. But the terrain soon turned rocky; Ghost led the way but the ground was unstable. A wrong move by him could send rocks and debris falling onto Seti, who was far behind him.

After several hours, Seti called to Ghost that he was tired

and needed to rest.

Do you mind if I keep going, Seti? I'm nearly at the top of the mountain and I think the fog is lifting!

Go ahead! You know where to find me!

Ghost proceeded to climb. He was doing his best to be extra careful, for fear of twisting a leg or worse, falling. With one of them already hurt, it could be disastrous if they were both crippled.

Finally, Ghost reached the gravelly summit and pulled himself up over the edge. The fog was drifting past him as the breeze gently blew. Overhead he could see the orange ball of the sun through the fog, and brief glimpses of the blue sky beyond.

Ghost turned toward the east and inhaled deeply. It felt good up here. The bird he had heard earlier – a hawk – made an appearance near his head and flew past him toward the sunrise.

As the fog cleared some more, the sun shone directly in Ghost's eyes, blinding him for a moment. But when his eyesight adjusted to the glare, he saw a most amazing sight.

There, nestled atop the next mountain range, was a castle.

The castle.

Ten

It was like something in a dream. Surrounded by a beautiful, snowy countryside, Neuschwanstein Castle was crafted from impressively massive blocks of grey stone, with three towers rising majestically over the landscape. It sat on an enormous outcrop of granite, acting as a foundation. There was a large stone-mosaic plaza before the gate house, granite steps leading to the square tower and a citadel in front of the court yard.

As the sun rose, the castle took on varying colors of pink, orange and white. On the exterior face of one wall were paintings of angels and clouds. Ghost gulped; every detail was exactly as his father had described it!

He was overwhelmed with emotion. All the stories he had heard, since he was just a young colt, every hope he had about this moment, every hardship he and Seti had suffered to reach this place – it all played out in his mind like a waking dream.

Seti!

Ghost had made his way down to where Seti was resting.

It's the most beautiful thing I've ever seen. Even better than what I imagined!

Let's go closer and see it the way your ancestors did!

—◦◦◦—

Every step they took across an open plain felt magical. The castle seemed to grow as large as the sky itself as they approached a stand of trees growing along its foregrounds.

My father said a battle was fought right here, in front of the castle! My ancestors fought bravely, alongside the soldiers!

It's so majestic, it makes me wonder why anyone would want to fight.

They continued through the trees and found a pathway leading into the castle courtyard. It was still early morning, and no one was around. They had the entire area to themselves. Seti didn't know where to look first, it was all so overwhelming.

I feel small...

Ghost couldn't stop looking up at the tall towers and spires. There were hand-carved stone figures scattered near the turrets and an enormous wooden drawbridge near the main entrance.

Seti, I'm going to wander around by myself for a while, if you don't mind.

I understand.

Ghost felt as if he was sleepwalking. His body was tingling with excitement at every new discovery, each new view. The scenery was breathtaking, too. Mountain ranges, snow-capped peaks, valleys that stretched as far as the eye could see. Without thinking, Ghost began speaking aloud.

Father, I made it. I'm here; at the place you told me about so many times when I was young. You gave me this dream of adventure…and a connection to my past. I've always felt as if I was part of something greater than myself…thanks to you.

He came around a corner and found a stone sculpture of a soldier – atop his horse. Ghost felt his heart pound. He moved closer; the stone horse looked exactly like his father.

Ghost heard a noise coming from the courtyard. He turned and was amazed to see faint, shimmering images of horses and soldiers – as if he was gazing at them from behind a gauze curtain. They were specters – visions of Ghost's ancestors that had graced the castle grounds in times long gone.

Ghost could hear an echoing click-click of the horses' hooves as they moved in military formation and the crisp snap of the flags carried by the soldiers, whipping in the breeze. Next came a long procession of proud horses bearing shining silver armor, followed by a row of dignified horses carrying royal coaches. His heart raced as they moved past him in a kind of spirit-parade; he knew what he was seeing wasn't real, but at the same time, he wanted to rush forward and join the otherworldly march.

As suddenly as the apparitions had appeared, they vanished. Tears came to Ghost's eyes. In an instant, he felt the presence of his parents, standing next to him, as the reality of the moment settled in.

Ghost, are you all right?

Seti had found him and walked to the sculpture.

Look, Seti!

I see…it's amazing.

Ghost nodded. Overwhelmed with gratitude, he bowed his head and looked at Seti with thankful eyes.

I'm so grateful for all of it…and I want to dedicate our journey to my ancestors and my parents. To my family…and yours, Seti. It's dedicated to Ramses.

Seti nodded and brushed up against Ghost.

Thank you, my friend.

They remained on the castle grounds for the rest of the day. It was possible for them to stay longer, but there was no need. Reaching the castle had completed their quest. The circle had finally closed; their adventure was complete.

They ate and drank their fill that night, down in the valley below, and recounted stories of their grand adventure. They laughed at the antics of the loon and recalled the terror they felt when they stumbled upon their first locomotive. The sights and sounds had been so different from what they were used to back in their own homes.

And yet, some things remained exactly the same. Their friendship; their love of family; their respect for nature and other animals. They realized that some things in life will be forever changing, but the ones that matter never will.

The next morning – a crisp and clear winter day – Ghost took a final look at the castle and then, alongside his best friend, began the long journey home.

There would be many more adventures for these two intrepid travelers – another epic sea voyage; a heart-pounding Arctic detour; a desperate race against time to stop a new and dangerous foe; and a visit to a most remarkable jungle where birds can sing in three-part harmony.

But those are stories of another time and place. For now, we bid bon voyage to two unlikely friends – the wolf and the Warlander – who set out to find adventure and ended up finding themselves.

MANNHEIM STEAMROLLER

THE WOLF & THE WARLANDER

CHARACTERS

PEGASUS: Ghost's Father
LADY: Ghost's Mother

GHOST: The Warlander
ECHO: His Mate
RIDER, SKY & DANCER: Ghost & Echo's Offspring

SHADOW: Seti's Father

SETI: The Wolf
LUNA: His Mate

RAMSES: Setti's Son
RAFF: Son of Ramses

CHARACTERS IN BOOK THREE
THE LONG ROAD

The Loon
The Circus Horse
The Milk Wagon Horse
Odessa The Angry Old Horse
The Donkey

GLOSSARY

APPALOOSA – Known for its spotted coat and incredible speed, the Appaloosa's striking appearance has been memorialized on cave walls dating back thousands of years.

CANTER – The easy three-beat gait of horses. A canter is a natural, loping movement, faster than a trot but not as fast as a full gallop.

FOAL – A young horse.

FRIESIAN – Originally bred in the Netherlands, these strong animals were used as draft horses, carrying out heavy chores on farms and in construction work. They were also used to carry armored knights into battle.

GALLOP – It is a beat gait, and the fastest gait for any four-legged animal.

MUSTANG – Descendants of the horses brought to the Americas by the Spanish, the Mustang developed into a free-roaming breed that became known for its impressive speed. It is also the general term for a wild horse – a "mutt" if you will.

NEUSCHWANSTEIN CASTLE Built by the shy King Ludwig II of Germany, as a refuge against public appearances, the castle is now a tourist destination popular for its incredible architecture and breathtaking views. King Ludwig II, a huge fan and supporter of German composer Richard Wagner, had a bedroom in Castle Neuschwanstein with paintings from Wagner's opera "Tristan and Isolde". This castle was also the one that Walt Disney modeled his famous Disney castle after, as seen in the Disney film logo.

RABIES – A contagious and fatal viral disease of dogs and other mammals that causes madness and convulsions, transmissible through saliva to humans.

STORM SHADOW – Born in 2007, this Buckskin Warlander stallion, now owned by Chip Davis, has won championship titles dating back to his first year in competition. He has astonished the breed world with these early victories, having bested top horses along the way.

TROT – A two-beat gait in which a horse moves at a pace faster than a walk, lifting each diagonal pair of legs alternately.

ABOUT MARK VELENTI

Mark Valenti has written dozens of television shows and movies in a career that has spanned more than 25 years, and his work appears on every major network and cable channel around the world.

He wrote *The Christmas Pageant,* a holiday romantic comedy starring Melissa Gilbert, for the Hallmark Channel, *Menno's Mind,* starring Billy Campbell, for Showtime, and *Like Father, Like Santa,* starring Harry Hamlin, for ABC Family. Among his many children's TV shows: *LazyTown, Back to the Future, Olivia, Gaspard and Lisa, Totally Spies, My Friends Tigger and Pooh* and *Julius Junior.*

He scripted the annual holiday special, *Mannheim Steamroller's The Christmas Angel,* for NBC, and served as Creative Manager for Disney Interactive. He was Story Editor for Nickelodeon's popular block of animated shows including *Rugrats, Catdog, Hey Arnold!, Rocket Power,* and *The Wild Thornberrys.*

Prior to his writing career, Valenti was Vice President of Development for John Hughes Entertainment during the production of *Home Alone* and *Christmas Vacation.* He began his entertainment career with a two-year stint at Steven Spielberg's Amblin Entertainment, followed by several years as script analyst for Ron Howard, Oprah Winfrey and Sydney Pollack's production companies.

For Kristen, Zach and Noah